The dead end of cruelty

Mason Searle

Contents

1. The outset of dread

The future was like a wild beast in this uncivilised world—untamed and unpredictable. The days and hours ahead were like a blank canvas only waiting for uncertain destinies to paint it.

Att started to move towards her twin brother Kei as she spotted him among the busy crowd at the airport. Her pulse pounded with anticipation as she made her way through the crowd in anticipation of seeing her brother and confidant again after two long years away.

Kei, who had recently returned from Turkey, was standing there enjoying the light from the pole. The yellow light caught the black hair's glitter.

Att finally caught up to him and gave him a playful arm-bump. He grimaced to simulate pain, but his broad grin revealed his actual feelings. Salutations: "Welcome back!" Att shouted, unable to control her happiness.

Kei replied with a voice brimming with warmth and affection, "It's good to be back."

The twins stood out from other people thanks to their stunning black hair and piercing red eyes. They stood out from the crowd and attracted onlookers' attention.

Kei possessed a calming personality that made him a natural beast tamer, whereas Att was noted for having a short fuse and being fiercely determined.

It didn't take him long to run into Naveah, who was unaware of his feelings for her. She had been his childhood sweetheart for as long as he could remember, but he had never told her about it because he was too bashful. Years later, he would finally have the chance to get in touch with her and perhaps even express his feelings.

He gobbled the food in front of Naveah with a frenzied hunger, and she observed him with a mixture of worry and amusement.

Kei was captivated to Naveah's easy humour and dazzling eyes as they conversed and caught up on old times.

She inquired, a tinge of mocking in her voice, "Do you need a second?" She said something that caused Kei's cheeks to flush, and he realised he must have been eating the dish too quickly.

In an effort to restore control, he nervously rubbed the back of his skull.

He said, feigning a smile, "No, I'm OK.

"Mmhm?" With a dramatic side-eye, Att gave him a quick glance.

"Hey wh-" A loud crash from inside the restaurant distracted them just as Kei was ready to change the subject and diffuse the tense atmosphere.

The three of them spun around to see two men fighting viciously, in what appeared to be a struggle to death rather than just a minor altercation. They discovered, to their horror, that those nearby were making no attempt to interfere.

Instead, they were using their phones to either watch or record the violence.

The first to respond was Att. She loudly slammed the table as she got out of her chair and went aggressively towards the altercation, her face etched with rage. After a brief moment of hesitation, Kei and Naveah followed her, examining the area for any potential threats.

Att became more and more enraged as they got closer to the two men. "Hey! She screamed, her voice rising above the clamour of the melee.

Naveah said, "Hey, Att, calm down," but she didn't hear her because her attention was on the fight.

Is this a circus performance? She screamed across the diner, "Why are you recording instead of stopping them?"

When Att reached out to grab the men who were on the ground in an attempt to break up the fight, she trembled in fright. Everyone in her immediate vicinity gasped in shock as they witnessed a scene that was beyond their wildest dreams.

The man on the ground was eating from the neck down and was immobile, his eyes gazing blankly above. A thick, disgusting white fungus appeared to be covering the surface of the other man who had been hitting him.

Some of the diners fled the restaurant screaming because they couldn't bear to look at the scene, while others stood motionless in horror and astonishment.

With her thoughts spinning from what she had just seen, Att stumbled backwards. Although she had witnessed some horrifying things in her life, this was something altogether different. She felt sick to her stomach just watching the man get eaten by the fungus.

The restaurant was silent for a short while, with only the sound of people's laboured breathing disturbing the silence.

As Kei comprehended what he had just seen, his heart was beating rapidly. The man on the ground had turned to face Att with a look of desire in his eyes, was covered in fungus, and was writhing in anguish.

"Att! With a voice choked with fear and worry, he yelled, "Get back!" quickly.

Att was quickly pulled away from the danger by Naveah, who also urged her to flee. Att's mind was spinning with incredulity as they sprinted out of the restaurant and found safety behind a nearby office building.

She asked in a shaky voice, "That was a...that was a zombie, wasn't it?

Kei grudgingly nodded.

He replied, his glasses beginning to cloud from the perspiration on his face. "I think so," he said.

What do you mean, do you believe that? It most certainly was!" she proclaimed.

More healthy people started to curl up in anguish, appearing to be possessed, as they gathered their breath and struggled to comprehend what they had just seen. Kei's head jerked in shock.

He mumbled, "They weren't even bit...how?" as he rubbed his brow in concentration.

Kei attempted to make sense of what was going on as they stood there, concealed from view behind the wall. Thoughts of possibilities raced through his head, but he couldn't get rid of the impression that something genuinely awful was playing out in front of their eyes. The three buddies realised they had to act quickly if they wanted to survive the night as the reality of their predicament set in.

The bitten ones are left dead on the floor, which is wrong, Naveah said, scarcely raising her voice above a whisper. They are not changing.

She could sense that something was very wrong from the folks groaning in pain all around them. She felt sick to her stomach because almost every aberrant one had strange white or off-white mushrooms growing on the surface of their skin.

The three pals were totally on their own because there was no information or forewarning about this circumstance. However, because of their familiarity with video games and movies, they were highly knowledgeable about the zombie apocalypse and how to survive it. But the circumstance they were now in was not at all like what they had seen in the movies. They had not anticipated it, and they soon saw they were in over their heads.

Kei couldn't help but feel regret as they travelled through the quiet streets.

He sighed, "I should've stayed in Turkey."

Att and Naveah turned to face him, their faces showing a mixture of worry and annoyance.

Att whacked him on the back of the head, jolting him out of his daydream, calling him a "selfish bastard."

Kei was aware that returning to the city had been a mistake, but there was no time to think about it right now.

"Let's leave the city and investigate the situation. Since there was no news, it doesn't seem like they've spread all that much," he remarked, attempting to control his voice.

Let's carry out that. Due to the lack of police protection and the seeming lack of danger, the two of them decided to go.

Kei, Att, and Naveah realised they had to remain composed and focused if they were going to survive the day's horrors. As they prepared to face them.

2. Inside the caged city

Southern CarolineThe atmosphere became gloomy, giving the area the appearance of being a portion of a destroyed building. It didn't smell as natural when the wind was blowing.

The three kept a low profile, going swiftly and stealthily through the deserted streets to Naveah's home. The fact that Naveah lived alone was beneficial in this circumstance. Her neighbourhood was tranquil and devoid of any indications of suspicious or infectious activity.

They exhaled a sigh of relief when they at last reached her home. They had, for the time being, reached safety.

They headed for the city's outskirts in Naveah's automobile. As they got closer to the boundaries, though, the tragedy only became worse. The three of them exited the vehicle with their mouths open and their eyes riveted on the massive walls and pits that were in front of them.

"What the hell is this?" With a tone of scepticism in her voice, Naveah exclaimed.

Att also struggled to believe what she was seeing. She shook her head in astonishment, "This can't be real," she whispered.

The entire city was encircled by iron walls, as though it were a cage. They were even more uneasy because there were no guards or police in the neighbourhood. They were clearly stuck and alone because all forms of transportation had been cut off.Saying "Att, Naveah!"Kei shouted for them to see the phone screen he was holding. His voice was filled with annoyance and rage when he realised even their communications had been disrupted: "Are they playing a sick joke on us?" They quickly understood that the government was somehow involved in the affair.

In an effort to comprehend the seriousness of the situation, Naveah sunk to the ground. It was difficult to comprehend how they had changed from conversing in a regular manner only a few hours prior to finding themselves stranded in an improbable situation with an odd sickness spreading throughout.

She voiced their perplexity by asking, "When did they even have time to build these walls?"

"Have you seen anything else?" Kei gave instructions while adjusting his spectacles and glancing quickly at the walls.Y es, nobody is in the room. Before the walls went up, they all most likely left. "But what did we do?" Naveah nodded. She objected.

They were silent for a brief period of time before Att said. "Perhaps we're being used as test subjects,"She caught Kei and Naveah's attention as Kei scowled and enquired, "Where did you get that idea from?"Did you see the fungus on the infected people's faces?" asked Att. Nearly all of them possessed it.But how does that relate to us serving as test subjects? Naveah persisted despite her unease.Kei and Att exchanged confused looks as they both turned to face her. I mean," Att paused, "I dunno. Is there any other way to describe this circumstance, though? Hasn't this been depicted in films? The Government experimenting out bizarre substances on selected individuals?"Indecisive as to what else to say, Naveah shrugged.

Att, this isn't a movie, Kei sighed. It is the truth. We can't just assume things without good cause, he said, placing his hand on her shoulder.

They were standing there, the strange calm heightening their senses, when they abruptly heard rustling behind Naveah. She swiftly got to her feet and moved in the direction of Att and Kei while scanning the area for any indication of danger.

As an infected slowly emerged from a neighbouring bush without running or groaning, the three of them all just stared. It was Naveah's immediate instinct to kill it, but they lacked any weapons.She said, "We have firearms in the car.Kei caught Att and Naveah's eyes.Kei sighed with exasperation. "Agh!

Why?" he questioned.Att stopped him in his tracks before he could act. Wait, let's watch it.Naveah had doubts. "No! We must avoid taking chances.There is only one, Att explained. The risk is not very high. Better if we keep an eye on it. If we're going to tackle this, we need to understand how they act.The infected appeared to be unaware of their presence and their whispered talk as they walked around, and they watched in silence from a safe distance. If they resembled zombies from films in any way, they would already have been found. The infected's response when it came into contact with a tree was even more unexpected. It started chewing on the bark as though it were food.

Naveah trembled at the scene. She muttered, "What the hell is wrong with it?"

Att said, "Kei, grab the shovel from the car," and Kei nodded as he silently brought two shovels.Naveah puzzledly turned to face Att. What are you going to do?" she enquired.

I'll make a noise to see how it responds. Kill it if it does. Att answered quietly.

Kei's head jerked in shock. "You're insane, but continue. He added, "We're here to save your ass," as Att turned and left after grinning at Kei.

Att approached the sick in an effort to obtain a better view of the peculiar fungus that was developing on its face. As Att drew nearer, the scent coming from the infected made her sick to her stomach and cover her nose.

To attract the attention of the sick, she suddenly stomped loudly on the ground. She was caught off guard and knocked to the ground as that thing suddenly sprang at her with a loud growl before she could blink."Att! Fuck!" To assist Att in regaining her equilibrium, Naveah cried out and tossed the shovel at the infected.

She exhaled and fought against it to maintain control of herself. Thankfully, there was no scratch or bite, although her left sleeve was torn.Kei sprinted over and gave the infected a quick kick to push it further away from them.But as it crept up on them, its horrifying mouth was open, like a racing bug. Separately, the three of them fled, and it pursued Kei.

Why am I always the one? The second shovel was still on the ground, so he stated as he took off his bulky trainers to use one of them as a weapon.But his shoes kept him alive because it was too busy tearing it apart to chase after Kei.Att and Naveah moved quickly. Att swung the shovel at the zombie's neck, slicing it open, because she didn't want to waste any more time. It yelled, fell to the ground, and black blood gushed from its nape.

Att let go of the shovel's handle gradually while puffing and panting hard. Kei and Naveah stared at the immobile body that was dripping with black fluid, paralysed in disbelief. They felt queasy as the foul scent of decay filled the air.

"Ugh!" Kei sighed.You all right? With anxiety in her eyes because Kei's comparison didn't look good, Naveah questioned. His eyes began to blur, and he started to perspire heavily."I'm.... I'm good.This fragrance annoys me. Let's get out of here, he said stuttering and struggling to stand up straight.

With their hearts still beating after their brush with the infected, the three of them made their way back to Naveah's automobile. Knowing they needed to rest and recuperate after the day's events, they made the decision to return to Naveah's house and spend the night there.The sky had already grown ominous as they travelled, throwing a sinister shadow over the barren countryside.

3. New arrival

Kei couldn't help but feel a sense of relief as they made their way back to Naveah's home. Being in a familiar environment helped ease his nerves, even if just a little bit. As the night went on, Kei began to feel a little better than before.

"Just great!" Suddenly, Naveah slammed a cabinet shut in the kitchen, causing Kei to jump. "What's wrong?" Att asked, looking up from the TV she was trying to connect but wasn't working, since the signal was cut off.

"I forgot to buy groceries since we were supposed to be out all day," Naveah replied, her frustration evident in her voice.

It was an epidemic situation. All of them were hungry after fussing about the infected all day. Att suggested they go to the store to get some groceries, "Why don't we just go and buy some? There's a store nearby. It's only 8.02 PM now." "You sure about that?" Kei yelled out from the other room as he was laying down. "You made trouble while we were with you. Who knows what you might do if I let you go with Naveah? I don't want her to get in trouble." Att stormed to the room

Kei was in and snapped at him, "Are you picking a fight with me?"No," he denied calmly. "I'm just stating the facts."

Att huffed and declared that she would go to the store alone. But before she could leave, Naveah stopped her. "You don't even know where the store is, do you?" she asked, raising an eyebrow.

Att hesitated for a moment before grinning. "I might.. . know?" she said, her voice trailing off uncertainly.Naveah sighed and went into the kitchen to get some knives and covers. "Wait for me, I'll go with you," she said to Att. Turning to Kei, she added, "Would you mind watching over the house while we're gone?"

Kei nodded, grateful for the chance to have some alone time. As Att and Naveah left, he settled back onto the couch and closed his eyes, letting out a deep breath. Despite the tension that had arisen earlier, he was glad to be in this peaceful, familiar place.

The silence of the night was almost too much to bear as Naveah and Att made their way to the store. The street lights cast an eerie glow on the empty streets, and the store was entirely neat and empty as if it had been abandoned for years.

As the two of them went about their business, choosing food and looking for weapons, they were completely unaware of the danger that lurked in the shadows. The infected moved in silence, unlike the zombies in the stories, and it was impossible to tell if they were nearby until they made a sound with objects.

Naveah was in aisle 4, filling her cart with as much food as she could carry. Att, meanwhile, was in aisle 9, searching for any weapons she could find, but the store was disappointingly devoid of anything useful.

Just as Att was about to give up, she heard a noise coming from the exit. She turned to see two infected shuffling inside, their eyes glazed over and their movements jerky and unnatural. Att's heart pounded in her chest as she realized that they were trapped, with no way out and no weapons to defend themselves.

As she took a step back to get to Naveah, her heart racing with fear and anticipation, a sudden gust of wind caught her off guard. She spun around, her eyes wide with terror, only to come face to face with a grotesque and unnatural horror.

The figure standing before her just a few inches before her, appeared to have been destroyed by some unspeakable force, its once-human features twisted beyond recognition. Its skin was covered in a writhing mass of eight-legged fungus, while its eyeballs had melted away into a sickening soup of pus and blood.

But worst of all was the stench that derived from this abomination. It was a putrid, nauseating smell that seemed to crawl into her nostrils and make its home in the back of her throat.

For a moment, she stood frozen, unable to move or even breathe. The horror before her seemed to be staring directly into her soul-one single move and she'll be dead.

She was only waiting for it to move away but she was getting at her limit as it got closer and closer.

As she was about to give up hope, without any warning, a sharp object pierced through the infected's vocal cords from behind, causing it to slump to the ground in slow motion, without any sound.

As she looked up, she saw him - her saviour. He stood before her with a gaze of piercing grey eyes that seemed to scan through her very being. His slender hands, wrapped in black gloves, held a dagger that was coated in the infected's black blood.

"Lone survivor?" He asked. "Huh? Oh! No, I have friends." Att was too taken by the moment.He threw out his gloves and offered her his hand, "Saijin."Att hesitantly took his hand as he uttered, "That's my name,""Att.." She repeated her name as well.The sudden realisation hit her as she panicked, "My friend is out here. She'll be in trouble. There are two more,"

Saijin walked closer to Att, his eyes fixed on her. The height difference was noticeable as he leaned in to whisper, "You don't know where you are, do you? There are not two, but a group surrounding the store. I was here peacefully until the two of you came and made sounds."

Att glared at him, but Saijin refused to waste any more time. "Where's your friend? Let's get her first," he said, taking charge of the situation.

"At Aile 4," Att replied, following Saijin quietly but quickly. They moved in a defensive position, ready to take out anything that might come their way.

As they made their way towards Aile 4, they spotted Naveah holding her knife near the drinks machine. It was clear that she had already become aware of their surroundings and was ready to defend herself.

"Att!!! I told you not to" She stopped midway, noticing Saijin behind her."Where did you pick that up?""Excuse me?" Saijin frowned and was about to say more but Att interfered."Hey! Relax, he saved me out there."

"I'll hear the details later, first let's get out of here."With that, they quietly moved near the entrance but Saijin all of a sudden put his hand out, motioning them to stop."We can't go further," he whispered. Att peeked out to see the entrance being blocked by them but there was no sound of their groan. They were only biting and scratching on the door and whatever was near them in silence. They followed Saijin near the exit since there were only two doors to get out of the store.

"We have to go through them, there's no other way. The exit has few of them. We might make it." Both of them opposed

Saijin's decision as they remembered the incident from that afternoon. But there was less time and options.

"Att can run fast, I'll distract them by converting their attention in the opposite direction and Saijin will wipe them off from the way."Naveah thought of a way that would be less risky than Saijin's as she grabbed the pan to use it as a distraction tool."depart on my signal, Saijin."

She moved further away from them and prepared herself to throw the pan. Att and Saijin's gaze fixed on her in a defensive position and finally, their awaited moment arrived when Naveah yelled out, "NOW!"

4. The 'fungus' within

Naveah let out the signal, "NOW!" and hurled the pan in the opposite direction of the exit near the entrance of the store. The loud clang of the pan hitting the ground caught the attention of the infected, and they rushed towards the noise, leaving the exit unguarded.

Saijin sprang into action, charging towards the exit and expertly slicing through any infected in his way. Att covered for Naveah, making sure that she was safe from harm.

As they fought their way through the infected, Att couldn't help but notice that Saijin was a professional at what he was doing. He moved with precision and agility, taking out the infected with ease. But they knew that they had to save their questions for later; they were still in the midst of danger.

Att had already observed that the infected were as fast as a cockroach when they were after their targets, but as slow as a snail at normal times. They used this knowledge to their advantage, darting past the infected with lightning-fast speed and making their way towards the exit.

"Let me get one!" Att exclaimed, launching herself at an infected in front of Saijin. However, she failed to pierce the knife in the right place and groaned as she felt her wrist twist from the pressure. The previous infected one she had taken down had been softer than this one.

"Who told you to act like a hero?" Saijin stepped in, finishing off the infected with ease.

"It's clear from here, let's go," Naveah said as she jogged towards them. They looked around and saw that the street was now clear of any infected. Saijin nodded and followed the two of them to Naveah's apartment.

Exhausted and relieved, the three of them slumped down on the floor as soon as they entered the apartment. They were covered in sweat and grime, their hearts still pounding with adrenaline from the intense encounter.

As they were busy catching their breath, Kei rushed over,"Are you guys alright? Or not." Kei paused as he noticed Saijin behind them."You are..?"

Saijin smiled as he took off his cap, revealing his brown hair. The light exposed the bangs near his grey eyes and his facial features clearly. Kei's eyes widened as he recognized the familiar face."Saijin...?" he uttered in disbelief.

Saijin nodded, a hint of a smile on his lips. Kei's agape mouth turned into a big grin as he reached out his fist towards Saijin, and he did the same. The two of them bumped fists, a sign of camaraderie and mutual respect.

"Didn't know we'll meet again like this." Saijin's lips curled into a smile and Att was left dazed."You two know each other?" "Yeah, we've been in touch since my group tour in Japan. He kinda saved me while hiking when I got lost." "He's Japanese? No wonder he looked Asian." Naveah said."I thought you were Kei at first, but when our eyes met, I was confused," Saijin said, turning towards Att."Is that why you saved me?" Att sounded annoyed."Kind of. I would've come a bit later if I knew." "This motherf-" Kei grabbed her mouth before she was about to say disgraceful words but then she paused, feeling the temperature of Kei's hand."Hey, why are you so cold?" "My head was burning so I used some ice cubes before you came," "Are you feeling okay?" "Yes, almost good. I was probably affected by the smell." He turned around and asked not seeing Naveah beside them,"Where's Naveah?"

"Will you guys eat and get to the point or just delay the situation by chit-chatting? We've got tons of shit to do." Naveah yelled out from the kitchen and her voice echoed in the room. "Yes, mam," Kei replied as he went inside to help.

After having plenty of food, they sat together, to sum up all the information they had gathered.

"Hold on! First," Naveah turned towards Saijin, "Full introduction please."

Saijin looked at her from across the floor, his arms crossed near his chest. "I'm originally from Japan but living in the US.

I'm 23 years old, and if you're curious about how I'm skilled at using weapons, I had military training for three years."

Naveah nodded, impressed. "That's cool, junior army," Att shrugged, but her voice was laced with jealousy.

Kei chuckled at their reactions. "Saijin's got some serious skills. You should see him in action."Saijin grinned, looking slightly embarrassed by the attention. "Just basic training."

"Let's get to the point then." Att fixed her composure, trying to change the topic, "According to my points, it's the government's doing, and we're among the test subjects."

"Have you ever heard of Alfred Russel?"Everyone's gaze turned to Saijin as he uttered an unknown name, meeting eyes with Att. "Who is that? Scientist?" Naveah asked."Brace yourselves," Saijin smirked, "'cause you're about to hear the mad part." "Just get to the point."

Saijin began to explain the theory he had learned during his military training.

Ophiocordyceps unilateralis, commonly known as the zombie-ant fungus, is an insect-pathogenic fungus that was discovered by the British naturalist Alfred Russel Wallace in 1859. It's known for its ability to infect and control the minds of ants, causing them to become zombie-like creatures that spread the fungus to their colony.

Alfred warned that the fungus was becoming stronger and had the potential to affect humans. He tried to raise awareness about the fungus during his time, but his warnings had been largely ignored.

Recently, when the Fungus seemed to have reacted as Alfred said, the Government biologists decided to experiment on a city with few people in it and unfortunately, the four of them became victims of the experiment, and now they're stuck in this post-apocalyptic world.

"Back when I was in the military, I heard them talking about the operation they were holding." Saijin continued, "I couldn't understand what they meant but the incident today explains a lot."

The room went completely silent as they fixed their eyes on Saijin. They couldn't believe what they were hearing. Something like fantasy on a TV show actually existed in real life and was happening to them. It wasn't as normal as it sounded. The fear and creep crawled over their body, leaving them shocked."...I was right," Att muttered."But why would the Government perform something openly like this? It's too cruel..." Kei clenched his teeth.

"Cruel to us! But a solution to them. Do you think our deaths affect them? No!" Att hissed under her breath.

Naveah asked Saijin, "Is there anything else you know? How is it spreading? If it's not something that spreads with bites, like a zombie."

Saijin thought for a moment before responding. "I'm not quite sure about that yet. But as much as I've observed so far, they're not undead. The bitten ones are dead, but the fungus spreads within their body and takes control over their nervous system."

"So they appear alive..." Att finished the sentence.

Saijin nodded. "Yes, but not all of them. The ones that were badly bitten died, but they appear to be moving due to the fungus."

Naveah looked horrified. "That's terrifying. So how does it spread?"

Saijin shook his head. "I'm not sure about the exact mechanism of transmission. It could be through contact with bodily fluids or possibly airborne transmission. We need to be careful and take precautions to avoid getting infected."

As they were listening, no one heard anything from Kei. Att glanced behind from her left shoulder to check on him, but he wasn't looking good."Hey hey, Kei! You alright!?" Kei took a deep breath. "I'm.....I'm fine. My stomach is acting up again." "Jeez, go take a rest. Are you having diarrhoea or something at a time like this?" She teased him."I'm not!!" He exclaimed after taking a peek at Naveah and flushed from embarrassment. As he got up to leave the room, he could feel his vision getting blurry. "Should I get you some green tea?" Naveah walked towards him. "Sure.""Att, take care of the rest. I'll help out Kei." Naveah said before leaving with him,"Got it!"

Kei sipped his mug, feeling a bit refreshed by the warmth of it while Naveah watched him from beside him.

"Is there something on my face?" Kei asked, noticing her gaze.Naveah chuckled. "Just a red flush."Kei tried to hide it. "It's the smoke."She looked at him with concern. "Are you feeling better now?""A little," Kei replied, still feeling a bit shaken by their recent encounter with the infected.

As they stood on the balcony, looking out into the darkened city, Kei felt his heart hammering against his chest. He realized that he and Naveah were alone, and the romantic atmosphere made him want to confess his feelings to her. But he also knew that it wasn't the right time. They were all busy thinking about survival, and he didn't want to complicate things by bringing up his personal feelings.

"Kei..." Naveah called out to him, her voice tinged with concern.

He turned to her, hearing the urgency in her tone. He saw Naveah staring at him with a frown. "Take off your glasses," she said."My glasses?" Kei hesitated for a moment but eventually took them off.

His heart almost exploded when Naveah moved closer and leaned near his face, her hands grabbing his chin. "Kei...your eyes," she said, her voice trembling.

"W-what's wrong with them?" Kei blinked in frustration.

"They've gotten blurry," Naveah said, her voice barely above a whisper.

Within a second, the worst fear encircled both of them, and their hearts tangled in terror as Naveah muttered, "This can't be..."

5. Incoming Fear

Att was sitting across from Saijin who seemed calmer despite the situation they were facing. "About the theory you talked about," she began, "do you have any idea how the fungus got here?" "No, I only explained as much as I knew."

Att's curiosity wasn't treated as she knew a little about these fungi diseases and how they spread through touch, food and stuff. She knew it was riskier for them to stay in that city for long. She felt as if the air was enough to kill them by the time.

Both of them agreed on the point that they had to escape from the city as soon as possible. But the walls they've dug up as borders won't be easy to climb out or break a path through them. What's more, they didn't know what was waiting for them outside the border.

"I want you to teach me how to use weapons. Rifles and daggers. Never used a real gun before." Att broke the silence as Saijin looked at her, studying her expression, and nodded,"Do you have one?"

"No, but we should set out tomorrow morning and get-" Att's words got cut off as Naveah walked inside the room. "This is bad!" She exclaimed. "What happened?" Saijin asked. "Kei...so mething's wrong with Kei's body."

Saijin and Att exchanged worried glances, and both of them strode towards Kei, who was still sipping on his tea. He sighed and turned to them, as Att observed Kei's red orbs turning into dirty maroon, his skin had gotten paler, and the white surface on his forehead was now clear. Her heart sank as she squeezed her lips tight, knowing what has happened. Her brother standing before her was infected by the fungus.

"I wonder how I'm still alive..." Kei chuckled to himself, "Maybe I'm the protagonist." His gaze was fixed on the cup on his hand.

"This isn't a joke!!" Att was about to launch at him, but he stopped her, holding up a hand.

"Don't come closer. This might affect you," Kei said, his voice strained.

The three of them halted, not knowing what to do or how to react until Kei spoke up.

"I would go out there and blend in with the other infected, but I'd rather stay here and let you use me as a test subject so you can survive out there," he said, looking up to meet their gazes. "Since my brain and nerves are still working fine. If things start to go south, don't hesitate to-"

"Shut your goddamn mouth!" Saijin yelled, cutting him off. "How are you so sure you're infected? It could be something else."

"How would you explain these on my forehead, my eyes, and the way my body is feeling?" Kei pointed at his skin and eyes.

"Then why are you still normal, unlike those who transformed Instantly?" Naveah spoke up.

"I don't know! Maybe there are other people similar to me, who were late to transform."

"Listen here, douchebag!" Att gritted her teeth. Even though she was trying to hide it, the fear and pain were visible in her eyes as she growled, "You're not infected, you're perfectly fine and no one-" she turned around facing Saijin and Naveah, "No one is allowed to talk about this any further. We'll get the info that we need, do what we need but no one mentions it!"

She glared at Kei from her left shoulder one last time and warned him before storming off,"If you dare say one more time that you're infected, I'll kill you myself!"

The three of them were left stunned, knowing Att was really worried and angry. No one could tell what the cause was, and every one of them felt fear inside of them, thinking they also might be affected like Kei.

As for Kei, he wasn't sure how much time he had left. But he decided to make use of the time he had left to experiment on himself, trying to understand the cause of the infection.

He was fighting with himself, trying his best to stay sane. He could feel his brain getting clouded from time to time, his stomach curling in moments, and his vision growing blurrier by the hour.

He got a different room and locked himself up inside there for the night, even though Att protested he shouldn't. As much as time passed, he could feel his condition getting worse.Abruptly, there was a knock on Kei's door, and he heard Naveah's voice. "Will you let me in?"

Kei hesitated for a moment, unsure if it was safe to let her in. "Don't...I don't want to take risks. What is it?" He walked closer to the door, placing his left ear against it to listen.

"I made some cold coffee...I know it's not time for a drink, but at least we should appreciate our time together," Naveah said.

There was silence for a few moments until Kei finally spoke up. "Leave it on the floor, I'll take it."

"Don't be like this. I already touched you! There's nothing wrong with it," Naveah replied.

Kei's heart sank as he realized that he might have already infected Naveah. "Naveah, that's the thing that's terrifying me. I don't even know what I've done..."

As Naveah stood outside the door, she could hear Kei's shaky voice. He was suffering slowly, worried that he had done something terrible to them. What if they were also infected because of him, since he had been beside them?

"You know I love cold coffee, right?" Naveah asked, trying to ignore the situation. "My mug is getting warm. So please take your coffee so it doesn't get warm. I want to drink with you."

After hesitating for a moment, Kei slowly opened the door to see the mug on the floor. "Don't worry, I'll drink while leaning on the door, since you're worried," Naveah said, sensing his hesitation.

There was no moon in the sky, and Kei's room was pitch dark, but he felt more comfortable in it. Naveah was sitting outside the room, resting her back against the door as she took a sip of the cold coffee. Att and Saijin were busy preparing for the next morning. Even though there were people around him, Naveah still felt the atmosphere was eerie.

"How does it taste?" she asked, gazing at the twirling foam on her coffee.

".....It's really good." Kei's voice was low and grasped as he replied, "You always made the best coffee."

Naveah chuckled and stood up to leave. "Don't worry! When we're out of here, I'll make Starbucks for us. The best one you've ever had."

Kei only managed to smile, but he couldn't answer. As he heard Naveah's footsteps fading away, he put the cup down and smiled at it.

"I'm sorry, Naveah. I lied," he muttered as he felt his vision getting blurry again, "I lost my sense of taste."

6. Onto another Discovery

The night seemed to pass by in a flash as Att, Saijin, and Naveah made plans to enter the Fort Jackson- a training centre for the army. With no police or military presence in the city, it was the ideal place for them to acquire weapons and practice their skills, unless it was squirming with infecteds.

They didn't hold out much hope of finding any significant clues about the government's motives, since they would never leave any clues behind. However, Kei decided to stay at the apartment and asked them to bring back heavy cover-ups and masks for him. They agreed, knowing it would be for the best.

As soon as they stepped outside, their eyes were met with the sight of countless drones hovering in the sky, scanning the area. It was evident that the government was monitoring the situation closely.

Att's anger boiled over at the sight of the drones, "These fucking pests!" She wanted to grab those drones and smash them into pieces but they were way too high for her to reach. It would be a futile effort.

Instead, she defiantly flipped the middle finger at every drone that passed by as they made their way towards Naveah's car. It was a small act of rebellion against the oppressive government that had abandoned them to the mercy of the zombies.

Her quiet apartment wasn't quiet anymore, the infecteds were roaming around there too, but they were far away to notice them. As they started driving, two drones began to follow them."I'm gonna-" Att was about to stand up inside the moving car but Saijin stopped her. "Stay down! Don't react. We'll break them when they get close enough."Just when Att converted her eyes from the drones, Naveah yelled out, "Saijin!"

Saijin slammed on the brakes with all his might, but it was too late as four or more zombies suddenly lunged at the car, with one of them being flung away by the impact. The sudden noise of the brakes attracted even more zombies in the area, and they started to converge on the car."Fuck!" Saijin quickly took control of the driving stick, "How much can your car handle?" He asked Naveah."Huh?" Before she could say anything, he floored the accelerator, pushing the car to its limits as they broke through the crowd of zombies.It was a tense and harrowing drive as they attempted to outrun the undead horde, but those grossed brainless figures continued to pursue them relentlessly, along with the drones that had been following them all along.

"How much longer until we reach the camp?" Att asked, struggling to remain seated as the car shook violently."I think ten minutes away!" "My car's gonna break at this rate. It's the only thing we've left." Naveah yelled from the backseat."What do you want me to do? Slow down and die?" Saijin exclaimed as he made a sharp turn and Att was thrown against the window, causing a hairline crack to appear. "Dude!" she exclaimed, rubbing her sore shoulder.

"Sorry, We're here!" He said, bringing the car to a sudden halt as they reached their destination. He quickly unbuckled his seatbelt and jumped out of the car, eager to get to safety.As they got out, they noticed the huge crowd rushing over. But thankfully, they had made it inside the training ground.

"Quick, close the gate!" Naveah yelled as she made a dash towards the gate of the training ground. Saijin and Att raced to catch up with her, and together, they managed to reach the gate just in time to slam it shut, managing to close it before they reached there.

Breathless and panting, they leaned against the gate and looked ahead to see a few of the infected walking around on the ground, further away from them, not in a pose of immediate threat.

Saijin quickly pulled out his daggers to glance at them,"Aim for the cords. One at a time," He uttered, and with a nod of agreement, the three of them dispersed, each taking on a target.

Att rushed towards the closest infected, channelling all her strength into a swift strike that sliced through its neck in one clean motion and moved away to avoid the spurting blood. She flinched at the sight and smell of the blood that sprayed out, feeling sickened by the gruesome scene.

She glanced at Saijin and as expected he was already done with three of them and was heading inside. The advantage they had there was- unlike Zombies, these infecteds didn't rise from the dead. So it was easier to handle the situation if there were a few unless they noticed your presence.

"Let's go," Naveah said, wiping her knife on the motionless body on the ground that she just took down.

As they stepped into the armoury, the stale and musty smell assaulted their nostrils, causing them to cover their mouths to avoid inhaling the foul air. Saijin quickly turned on the lights, brightening the room and revealing a gruesome sight.

Their eyes fell upon a series of bodies lying on the ground, some of them covered in a white fungus, while others appeared to have been killed by other means. Some had those white fungus on them, some didn't."What the hell happened here?" Att uttered as they slowly walked past the bodies, towards the weapons.

Their attention was quickly drawn to the impressive array of firearms displayed on the walls: Gewehr 98, AK 74, AKM, FAMAS F1, HK416, StG 44, and M107, all decorated in the first box. As they moved further down, they spotted a few

M1911s, two Glock 19s, and a single M2 Browning machine gun.Despite the grim scene before them, obtaining these weapons was crucial to their survival.

"Why did they leave them here?" she wondered aloud, feeling a mix of excitement and curiosity as she brushed her hand against the impressive array of firearms on display. It was her first time seeing them that close. Saijin picked up the AK 74 and suggested that Att take the Glock 19. Naveah, on the other hand, aimed for the FAMAS F1 and walked over to the nearby daggers stock.

"Att, I found your options," Naveah called out, holding up a pair of sleek and deadly-looking daggers.Att peeked from behind and a huge grin appeared on her face as she joined Naveah, "Yes! Now we're talking. I prefer them over guns." she exclaimed, picking up two of the daggers and wrapping the belt around her thighs."Keep the gun too. You don't know where you might need that." Saijin shoved the pistol on her wrist and walked away as Naveah looked at her."Guess I'll keep a dagger too."

After selecting their weapons, the group continued to investigate the armoury. However, they soon realized that none of the Wakitoki devices or communication equipment was functional, and the signal had been cut off in the area too. Signs of fighting and struggle were evident on the walls, leaving them to wonder where the fungal outbreak had started from.

As they were exploring, Att noticed a drone approaching them."Saijin," She whispered, "Are you good at sniping?"He looked at her, confused ."What for?"She pointed upwards and Saijin didn't take a second to understand what she meant.Sai jin nodded, picking up the sniper to take down the drone's fan. It could be useful for them to get a signal or connection with them. He successfully shot down the drone, causing it to crash to the ground.Att grabbed it and turned the camera towards her, it was still working. She clenched her teeth and hissed, "Having fun watching the show Bastards? Just wait for us there!" She hissed, moving her eyes closer to the camera, "Ya'll are fucked when we get out of this city." Before she could finish talking, the drone was switched off. "What the fuck? They turned it off!" She exclaimed.Saijin scoffed, "What did you expect? They'll keep it connected after what you said?"

She clicked her tongue in annoyance and pocketed the fallen drone, knowing it was still useful to them anyway.

As they were about to leave the armoury, the group suddenly heard a clunking sound from inside and paused. Before they could react, something smashed Naveah's back with a sickening thud, causing her to crumple to the ground with a loud groan."Argh!" she screamed out, writhing in pain." Hey-"Saijin turned around just in time to face that maniac smile on that half-melted face of the guy before him, striding towards them, swinging a baseball bat that scraped against the ground.

7. Moments of Decay

The apartment was completely empty without Naveah, Att and Saijin. Kei sat cross-legged on the bare floor, his eyes closed, and his mind deep in thought. He had covered every inch of the apartment's windows with thick curtains, blocking out the sunlight that made him feel uncomfortable and frustrated.

As he sat there, he noted every feeling and movement within his body. It was evident that the fungus despised heat, but he was still unable to understand why he had been affected by it. He raised his hand and looked at his palm, observing as his pulsed veins were seen through the thin skin. It was a miracle, that his mind was still functioning, given the state of his body.

Desperately searching for a clue, Kei tried to think of a situation that was different from the ones he had experienced with Naveah and Att on the day it all began. After what felt like an eternity, he finally remembered something - the food. Att and Naveah only drank, they didn't get a chance to take a bite since the commotion happened and he was the only one who ate. The restaurant was the place where the plague began.

"Could it be..." Kei mumbled to himself, deep in thought. Abruptly, he felt a sharp pain in his head, as if something was sucking out his brain. "Arrghhhh!!" He screamed out in agony, clutching his own shirt to the point of ripping it apart. He was grateful that there was no one around to witness him in that condition.

The pain lasted for only a few seconds before lowering, leaving Kei gasping for breath and caressing his forehead. He turned to the mirror to observe the growth of the fungus, which had spread greatly since the last time he had checked. It was like a parasite, slowly sucking the life out of his body and taking control of his brain. Kei was a victim of this slow-motion attack, but why was he different from others? The question lingered in his mind, unanswered.

In the [Jackson Fort]-

"Naveah!" Att quickly squatted down on her knees and grabbed Naveah, asking urgently, "Can you stand?"

"I...I can!" Naveah replied, closing one eye and breathing heavily from the pressure. Her spine felt broken as she tried to stand up, leaning on Att for support.

Their minds were filled with terror as they watched an infected man walking towards them, wielding a baseball bat. He wasn't normal, and he could see them. Just when things couldn't get any more surprising, he spoke up, "Woah! What a lame expression you got there!"

Saijin's eyes widened in shock as he heard the guy talk. "What are you?!" he asked, fear creeping into his voice.

"What am I?" The infected guy paused, his grin fading away for a split second and returned with an even wider grin. His dark, empty eye sockets were clearly visible as he looked up and shouted abnormally, "I wonder what I am!"

He launched himself at them with a maniacal laugh, filling the area with his terrifying presence. Saijin was paralyzed with fear as he tried to come up with a plan to defend himself. Just then he heard Att's voice,

"Saijin! Duck!!" With Att's signal, he quickly bent down, avoiding the insane guy's attack. Att aimed her daggers at the man, hitting him in the chest and shoulder. "Ow ow ow ow!!! I can feel the pain, you wench!" he glared at Att, making her flinch from a distance.

But seeing his attention moving away, Saijin took the initiative to wrap his belt around the man's mouth and pin him down to the ground. He struggled to get free from Saijin's grip, but the daggers made him weak. His voice was muffled.

"Are you infected or not? Answer with your head, or I'll blow it off!" Saijin warned him, pointing the rifle at his head. His grey eyes gave off a warning sign, and it wasn't a bluff. Saijin was ready to shoot if he saw any wrong move, and the man on the ground valued his life as he nodded vigorously.

Saijin took off the belt from his mouth, and the man gasped for air. "I'm-I'm not infected. Not infected," he said in a panicked voice.

Att strode over and stood before him, her shadows looming over him. He squinted his eyes and looked up to meet Att's gaze. "What's yo-" Before he could finish, Att aimed for his jaw and landed a hard kick with her boots, causing him to flip over to the other side, loosening from Saijin's grip.

"Woah! Att, down girl! He's human," Saijin said as he patted her shoulder and walked over to the guy. "Don't try anything funny and spill the beans. Explain these on your face," he said, pointing to the growing fungus on his neck and his missing eye.

"I'm taking Naveah to the car," Att said, firmly grasping Naveah's arm.

"I'm fine. I was enjoying the show," Naveah replied, but Att wasn't having any of it. "No, the heat isn't good. Let's get there!" She pulled Naveah along and glanced at Saijin over her left shoulder. "And deal with him, or else I might become a murderer."

Saijin scoffed and bent down on his knees to face the guy, "What's your name?"

That guy sat up and shook his head, playing a smirk on his face. "Why? You're interested in me?" Seeing how Saijin's face remained expressionless, he felt lame about his own joke and replied, "Kyle."

"Okay, Kyle! You'll have to come with us!" Saijin said as he began wrapping his fists with the belt.

"Hah? Who said I would?" Kyle replied, his arrogance showing.

"That wasn't a request," Saijin said firmly before landing a fatal hit on the back of Kyle's neck, rendering him motionless on the ground. However, carrying him to the car was risky. Saijin wanted Kyle because he was similar to Kei, and there must be something Kyle knew. But interrogating him right there wouldn't be a good choice since the heat was getting insane, and there could be infecteds around somewhere.

"Is he dead?" Att walked near Saijin, shadowing her eyes with her palm.

"No, but we need him," Saijin replied. Att nodded, agreeing with Saijin. "Yeah, that's what I came here to tell. He's similar to Kei," she paused for a moment and then added, "No, Kei is saner than him."

"Is she alright?" Saijin asked, pointing at Naveah, who limped out of the car and was checking out the damages Saijin had caused.

Att sighed and shrugged her shoulders, looking away. "We're not done trolling the area yet."

Saijin nodded and spoke up, "I think there are more survivors out there."

"So? It has nothing to do with us," Att said, ignoring Saijin's point and starting to walk towards the main quarter. It was clear that, even though it was an epidemic situation, Att wasn't interested in taking any strangers among them, unless they were useful.

Although Saijin wanted to say something, he refrained from doing so after getting Att's hint of not bothering with it.

They didn't waste much time since Kyle was still unconscious on the ground with Naveah present around him. They couldn't take any chances with him regaining consciousness.

Quickly gathering their masks and plenty of gear, they shoved everything into a bag and rushed out. Saijin wore his gloves and covered Kyle with a long length of cloth to put him inside the trunk.

"Let's take a roundabout route and get a glimpse of what's happening in the city," Saijin suggested.Att nodded, and they set off, taking a detour to avoid the infected areas and get a better understanding of the situation.

As they drove through the city, the scene before them was nothing short of a nightmare.

The sky was a sickly shade of orange, casting an eerie glow over everything. The streets were littered with abandoned cars, some with shattered windows and others with doors left open, as if the drivers had fled in a hurry. The sidewalks were cracked, and weeds had taken over, growing wildly in every direction.The scene only got worse. The bodies of the dead littered the streets, some still in their homes, while others were left out in the open, rotting in the sun.

As they drove past the ruined buildings, they suddenly heard a faint voice calling out to them. Saijin brought the car to a halt and looked in the rearview mirror to see two young girls and a man rushing towards them."Please wait!!!" The girl shouted desperately, waving her arms in the air."Fuck why is she yelling?" Att said, looking around in panic, since her voice was loud enough to alert the infecteds roaming around there. And Att's fear became real when they saw the infecteds turning in their direction.

8. Gruesome Escape

The infecteds roaming around noticed them and started approaching their direction."Please let us in!" the girl outside begged, her desperation palpable as she pounded on the window.

Att hesitated. "Saijin, don't-" she was about to stop him,"Get in!" But he unlocked the car doors and the three of them squeezed inside.

"Watch out!" Naveah yelled as the Zombies started to rush in their direction.Saijin tried to back up the car and make a hard turn but that's when things went south. The car ran out of gas, and it screeched to a halt at the corner of the road.All of their bodies shivered in fear and their hearts were ramming at their chest as they cursed their luck."What're you doing? Start the car for fucks sake!" one of the girls beside Naveah panicked.

"It ran out of gas now, out of all the time?" the man sitting in the middle exclaimed.

Their car was now surrounded, with the infected attacking the trunk and windows. "It's gonna get worse if we don't do something!" Att threw her gun at the man, urging him to fight."You want us to fight these?" he asked, with widened eyes.

"What else? Just watch and die?" Naveah snapped, pushing an infected away and opening her door.

"I'll take the front!" Saijin took charge, declaring that he would take the front.

The two girls stayed in the car, watching them fight as they cleared the area by eliminating one by one, thinking it was getting safe.Just then the other girl clutched her arm and muttered with trembling in her voice, "Sister...."She followed her gaze and looked behind to see a flock appearing from the back and the number was larger than before.They sat there frozen, watching them rush over knowing it was the end for them, unable to run or survive.

As the infected crowd drew closer and closer, fear gripped her and her sister, seeing the horrendous groans and ap-pearance. She quickly closed the door and hugged her sister, squeezing her eyes shut. The man who had been fighting alongside Naveah and Att turned around to check on his daughters."Look behind!" he shouted, grabbing Saijin's arm. "Please help my daughters!"

Att and Naveah turned to see the horde rushing towards them, frozen in terror. Their wrists ached from the fight, but they knew they had no time to retreat.Just when the infected pounced on the trunk, Kyle kicked it open and rose up,"Agh! They had to put me in a--" he stopped midway as his eyes fell on the approaching crowd. A wide grin spread across his face. "Whooaah?! What do we have here?" He stood up.

"Kyle! Your bat is inside the trunk!" Saijin yelled out.

Kyle glanced at the trunk and picked up his bat."Hmm, should I smash them or...them?" He snickered, darting his eyes between the approaching zombies from the front and the group of humans behind him.

The zombies didn't attack him, so he stood there, watching them squirm around. "Well, I could make a feast from either side anyway!" he exclaimed, jumping into the middle of the ground with maniacal laughter. He continued to smash what-ever came his way, relishing the thrill of the fight.

The sight of Kyle mercilessly slaughtering the infected without any second thoughts, made the group stand rooted to the spot, unable to look away. But it wasn't enough.

"Let's back him up from here," Att said, pulling out her gun. Saijin and Naveah joined her, aiming their rifles.

But the number of infected continued to increase, and the group knew they couldn't hold out much longer.They were so busy shooting, that they didn't realise how far they'd backed away from the car, where the girls were.

"We can't stay here anymore! Att, get the bags and the girls," Saijin yelled out.

"But where can we go? Nowhere is safe around here," Naveah protested, struggling to keep her aim steady.

"You and your damn car. How could you forget to load it up too?" Att snapped, feeling her gun running out of bullets. "Fuck!"

"How is it my fault?" Naveah shot back.

Att quickly strode to the car and pulled out the bags."Get out and follow me," she ordered the girls, spitting out the words with anger and frustration as they scrambled out of the car.

Att was so focused on grabbing the bags that she didn't notice the zombie creeping up on the girls from behind. Suddenly, a blood-curdling scream pierced the air, causing her to turn around just in time to witness a dreadful scene.

The zombie had plunged its nails deep into the little sister's eyes, and cheeks, as it severed her neck half open, tearing her flesh apart and causing blood to spurt everywhere. The girl's gurgled cries for help echoed in Att's ears, "Sis...ter...kh," the blood sprayed on the infected's face as it continued to feast on her before their eyes."AAAHH!!! Simi!! NO! NO-" Before she could even separate herself from Simi's hand, another zombie lunged at her, with more following closely behind.

And Att was there, standing and watching with her widened eyes. Things happened quicker than expected and she was unable to move a single muscle as the blood-bath was playing right before her eyes.

The sound of bones cracking and flesh tearing was deafening, the stench of blood, and their screams of agony and despair echoed through the air, with their organs spilling out and their struggle for survival coming to a brutal end.Att almost stopped breathing, paralyzed by fear and shock, even when she clearly saw three of the infecteds approaching her to do the same they just did with the two sisters.

That's when someone pulled her by the collar and yanked her from behind, "Eiyoo if you wanna die then let me kill you first!" Att broke out from her horror and that maniacal smile flashed before her eyes as Kyle pierced his bat through the infecteds mouth.

Att finally snapped out of her horror and started panting, "They're...They--"

"Att!" Saijin called out, jogging towards them and halting in shock as he surveyed the bodies and Att's state. He noticed Kyle's grip on Att's collar and glared at him. "Did you do this?"

"Haah?! I just saved your little friend here!" Kyle said, tossing Att aside.

Their father rushed over, panic etched on his face. "Are my daughters safe?" he asked frantically.

"I--" Att began, but Kyle blurted out, "No, they're dead. And you all better keep moving if you wanna live."

"What?" the man scoffed, disbelief written all over his face. "Are you punks messing with me?" he growled, grabbing Saijin by the collar. "Where are my daughters?"

"Over there. Those bones are them!" Kyle continued to gaslight the man, provoking him until he launched himself at Kyle to beat him up. However, his punch landed on Kyle's infected area and within a few seconds, his body began to curl up as he let out a harsh scream.

"Tch, this is such a pain, pain!" Kyle muttered, tilting his head upwards. His grin had faded away completely, making him look almost human.

"Are you guys watching a drama or something, leaving me here?" Naveah rushed over and she caught on the scene of that man transforming into an infected, but his sense was still hanging there as he groaned unclearly, "Kugh...My..daught...aghrs.."

Without hesitation, Naveah spent her last bullet, putting the man out of his misery. Saijin nodded swiftly and grabbed Att's arm, whispering softly, "Let's go!"

They wasted no time and hurried out of the place, with Kyle clearing the path ahead of them. After several minutes of running, they finally found a hotel that wasn't swarming with infecteds and rushed inside the elevator, pressing the button for the 22nd floor. As they ascended, Att leaned against the elevator wall and took a deep breath, trying to forget the gruesome scenes she had just witnessed and started thinking about Kei.

"What has happened?" Naveah asked, unaware of what had occurred near the car.

Saijin let out a sigh, shaking his head and turned to Kyle, who was checking out his bat while whistling."I'll tell you later, but for now, stay away from him," he warned.

"We need to leave ASAP. Kei is waiting for us," Att spoke up, regaining her composure. "There were infecteds around Naveah's house, and we can't tell what might happen."

The elevator pinged, and the doors slid open, revealing a dimly lit hallway. Kyle stepped out first, blocking the front."I could've suggested something, but never mind," he said, cryptically.

"What is it?" Att asked, facing him.

"Hmm? Why should I tell you? Hahahahah," Kyle started laughing maniacally once again as he moved backwards. Finally, he stuck out his tongue and said, "Bye-bye," before turning around and rushing further down the hallway, running away from them.

"This little..." Att gritted her teeth and rushed after him, their footsteps echoing through the empty hallway. Naveah tried to grab onto Att, but she was too fast. Saijin joined her, and the two of them rushed after Att, as Saijin grumbled in irritation, "This isn't a time to play tag!"

9. Unforeseen

The dimly lit silence of the hallways of the hotel were shattered by the loud footsteps of four people trying to catch up to one another. Kyle began to jump down the stairs, leaping on the stair boundaries, as Att followed his steps at greater speed while the cold wind whipped her face. Before they could realize it, they reached the ground floor near the garage, and Kyle finally halted.

"It's a dead end, you br-" She paused before pulling out her dagger when she saw plenty of cars and bikes abandoned in the garage. There were dead bodies laying on the ground, some entirely covered in fungus as if the body never existed, some eaten half.

Saijin and Naveah also noticed the scene from behind. They slowly walked inside the dark garage and discovered most of the cars were damaged, broken, and scratched.

"You could've just said it normally that you're taking us to the garage, instead of making us run all the way down with panic," Naveah said as she brushed her hand against the broken Camry.

"Why should I? I was only running as I liked,""Why'd you say bye-bye then? "Provoking is fun~" Kyle replied with a wide grin as he glanced at Att.

"Guys! I found one without any damage," they heard Saijin's voice from the back of the garage and strode towards him.

"How is it?" Naveah asked.

"It's a Mustang. Top speed is 162 mph, thanks to the 5.0L V8 engine," Saijin said as he made himself inside the car and started the engine to test it out. "I guess we're good to go. Where's Att?"

They looked around to check on Kyle and Att, but they were out of sight. Within a second, an unspoken panic encircled them as Naveah rushed out of the garage, searching for them. What scared her most was Kyle getting out of sight; who knew what he might do to Att if she attacked?

Then she saw her, trolling around on the ground floor near the elevator, with Kyle following her from behind.

"What are you doing?" Naveah said with anger and a worried voice as she strode towards her.

"I thought I might look for some food since we're here. The shops are probably all ruined and affected by the fungus," Att replied.

Naveah sighed from relief and said, "Let's go together. I'll go get Saijin."

The three of them got into the elevator, leaving Kyle near the car, to search the hotel and see if they found something important or useful. They clicked for the 3rd floor since the reception area was there, but for some reason, the elevator didn't stop at the third floor and started ascending towards the 19th floor.

"W-what's happening?" Naveah asked, feeling panicked. They exchanged glances, and everyone was in a defending position, not sure what might appear when the door opened.

After what felt like an eternity, the door slid open with a ping sound on the 19th floor, and their eyes fell on Madelyn and Noelle, who were waiting for the elevator to arrive. They stared at each other for a few seconds, unaware of what to say. But then Noelle hopped on along with Madelyn as if it was nothing and closed the door.

All of them went to the 3rd floor, and it appeared they were also there for food and supplies. Noelle looked like a splitting version of Att, except for her brown eyes.

"Are you guys the only survivors in this area?" Naveah broke the silence and asked.

"I don't know about that, but we're in a group of 8 people," Madelyn answered.

"Any clue of what's happening?" Naveah asked again, trying to get to a point.

Madelyn let out a sigh and nodded, "The drones proved it all. We were chosen to be killed, what else?"

"Maybe we should join each other and find a way to get out of here," Saijin suggested.

"No!" The two silent members, Att and Noelle, declined immediately at the same time. "I don't want to add more people to our group and get betrayed again," Noelle hissed.

"Betrayed?" Naveah asked, her curiosity rising as she got the hint that something might have happened to them. It wasn't something unexpected since, in a critical situation, humans are willing to do whatever they could to survive.

"But at least it would be better if we exchange information to get some clues out of this place," Saijin suggested again.

"We don't trust strangers," Noelle took Madelyn's hand and walked away without further conversation, leaving Saijin shocked as he shrugged and walked back to the garage.

They were surprised to see Kyle waiting for them near the car politely.

"Wow! Looks like you really wanna be with us," Att said mockingly.

"Free food," Kyle replied.

"Are you addressing us as food? Or the real one?" Naveah asked.

"Who knows~?" Kyle said as the wide grin appeared on his face again.

As they piled into the car, Saijin revved the engine and the car was completely fine to go. Their hearts were heavy with worry for Kei, who had been left alone at Naveah's apartment for hours.

As they approached the building without any hindrance on the streets, their relief turned to shock and horror. The street was lined with infected, their eyes glazed over as they moved towards Naveah's apartment. "What's happening here?" Naveah said with horror in her voice. When they moved closer, they met with a scene of devastation. Flames licked hungrily at the walls of the building, casting a spooky orange glow across the surrounding area. The heat was intense, and they could feel it beaming off the building even from several yards away.

"No! Kei is inside!" Att skipped out of the car, and without a second thought, rushed towards the building, as the others followed after her with fear and terror in their minds.

The intense heat from the raging fire had turned Naveah's apartment into a charred and blackened ruin. The thick smoke filled the air, stinging their eyes and making it difficult to breathe. The walls were cracked and crumbling, and the furniture was almost reduced to a pile of ash and burned remains.

As they cautiously made their way through the destroyed apartment, their eyes fell on Kei. He stood in front of the kitchen, his once-handsome face distorted by the hideous fungal growth spreading across his forehead and down his face. His mouth was smeared with blood, and his hands were coated in the same dark, viscous fluid.

At first, they thought he had transformed, but as they looked closer, they realized the black blood on his hands and face wasn't his own. Two lifeless bodies of the infected lay motionless on the ground under him, their throats torn open and blood dripping from their wounds.

Kei's gaze met with Naveah's, his eyes wide with fear and confusion. He struggled to speak, his voice shaking and barely audible, "Na...veah..?"

The scene was a dreadful display of a brutal reminder of the horrors that had consumed their world. The air was thick with the stench of burning flesh and the sickly smell of decay. It was a sight that would haunt them for a long time to come- a sight of their beloved person committing cannibalism.

10. Brief Elation

The sound of the fire's loud crackling and the house burning was nothing compared to the sound of their heartbeat as they watched Kei in silence. Kyle was analysing Kei's appearance until he finally spoke up, "He's passed the mid-phase. It's safe now, we should leave."

The walls were falling apart and they knew they needed to leave before it was too late. They quickly grabbed Kei and headed towards the car. "Are you feeling okay?" Att asked, handing him a towel and a change of clothes. Kei replied, "Yes. Are you guys alright?" He glanced at them, his glasses were broken, and his vision was impaired.

"We're a bit tired though. We had a lot of fights," Naveah tried to lighten up the mood. After exchanging glasses with Att, Kei could finally see better, and his eyes fell on Kyle, who was staring daggers at him. Kyle's situation looked similar to Kei, but he was stronger. "Who is that?" Kei asked, referring to Kyle.

"The thing that'll prove you're perfectly fine?" Att answered. "Who are you calling a thing!?" Kyle clicked his tongue."...Are you trying to prove that Kei also has a screw loose?" Naveah meddled, "Cause this guy isn't perfectly fine at all."

"Are we going to chit chat here? Because we're having more guests coming over," Saijin interrupted them, pointing out the infected roaming around. The house was no longer there, and they needed another safe place to stay. They decided to go to the hotel from last time.

As they hopped inside the car, Att pulled out the drone and asked Kei if he could find something useful in it. Kei, being an expert at electric systems, took the drone and scanned it, only to find that it was switched off. "No! All we can do is charge our phones," Kei said, handing Naveah a wrapped package. She opened it to find all of their phones, perfectly fine, but still no signal.

"Say, Kei... What happened back there?" Saijin finally broke out of silence and asked as he focused on the road. Kei was silent for a moment, then told them what happened. When he went downstairs to pack up after seeing the zombies approaching the building, he suddenly felt a deep pain in his head and screamed out loud. Following his scream, the zombies rushed inside, breaking the door, and Kei's instincts turned into a predator looking for prey. He couldn't resist stomping his teeth into those infecteds flesh. If there were humans or animals, he would've devoured them too. As if he didn't exist anymore in that body.

"The fungus reached your prefrontal cortex," Kyle spoke up, making all of them silent as they shipped their gazes to him. "Now it's a matter of time for them to spread within your whole brain function." All three of them were surprised as they heard Kyle talking. More than the information, what shocked them was Kyle talking about something that made sense.

"We're here, go up. I'll park the car," Saijin said as they went straight up to the 20th floor without meeting Madelyn or Noelle. It was almost evening, and the drones flying around were clearly seen because of their red lights. It had only been three days, but it felt like an eternity to them when they sat down in the room with no fear or trouble, comfortably.

Att and Naveah lay down with their faces flat on the bed. Then, Att stood up and looked at Kyle. "So what's with you?" she asked, pointing to his face. Kyle's infected eyes and neck were clearly seen under the light."What? What did I do?" He said, seeing Att staring at him. She pointed her finger to his face and signalled about the condition of his face with her hand."Tch.... I'm similar to uhh... Kei!" Kyle paused to see their attention towards him as if they were dying to hear his story, and he began.

Kyle was an anatomy student. Before all of this happened, they had a class on 'pithovirus sibericum' - a virus similar to the fungus. Hearing it had host control syndrome was suspicious, but he and his girlfriend still experimented on it.

That's when they learned about the process of their growth and reproduction - a splitting image of Cordyceps, the fungus spreading at the moment. That virus had three types - one spread within a minute, taking control of the host and sucking off their cortex sep. The second one was weak and made the host suffer bit by bit, spreading from vein to vein and reproducing every hour. And lastly, the queen of that species, the rarest one. It was impossible to detect before one week, and within that time, all the organs of the host had been already under their control, except for the heart. And when it reaches the heart, the host will stop breathing in a second and eventually perish as the ingrown parasites will peek out of every part of the hole in one's body.

"If you're saying that the virus was the same as the fungus," Att spoke up, "then that explains a lot. Kei and you are probably affected by the second type."

"But what was the cause?" Saijin asked.

"The food," Kei replied. "I found out when I was alone. They probably mixed the fungus with food in specific restaurants."

"What would they achieve from killing millions of people?" Naveah asked as she brought coffee and food for them and sat down. They all looked at each other with anger and a desire for vengeance. The situation was unacceptable.

"Power...Control," Saijin said as he cracked his neck. "So, there's no cure?"

"Not to my knowledge," Kyle shrugged. "But there could be one."

"There must be one!" Att said. "They wouldn't watch us without a reason. They're probably experimenting to figure out a cure."

They all nodded at Att with a glimmer of hope for finding a cure and helping Kyle and Kei. That small flash of hope amidst the plague felt as precious as a rare jewel.

The sky was getting darker and darker with every passing minute.As the group relaxed and laughed, Kyle's eyes wandered, and Att suddenly asked him, "Were you alone from the beginning? Where's your girlfriend?"

Kyle paused and looked away. "No, I had three best friends and my girlfriend. But guess what?"

"What what?" Att scooted over with curiosity.

Kyle turned to face Att with a wide grin on his face and uttered, "They're in my stomach now, probably getting digested! Kekeke," he snickered.The unexpected reply made everyone freeze. Kyle was giggling, but his eyes were filled with self-hatred, guilt, and rage. He stood up and walked out of the room, swinging his bat and whistling.

Att followed him to the rooftop, where Kyle stood on the edge of the wall. "You know, my foster father used to call me Brat! That was the first name given to me. And Kei named me Att from the last words of 'brat'. We ran away from our abusive foster parents at the age of 12," Att said, chuckling. "We were orphans. Kei and Naveah were all I had."

"So we all had issues, I see," Saijin said, approaching Att from behind, followed by Kei and Naveah to join them.

As the group reunited, they shared each other's backstories about how Saijin had to kill his own parents because they transformed, how he helped Kei in the mountains, and how Naveah had to live separately since her parents divorced. She didn't even know if they were alive or not.

As they bonded, Kyle watched them cheering each other up, from the edge and a single water drop slid away, without anyone's notice.

"Hey! Saijin give me your phone. Let's take a group picture. We'll frame it after getting out of here," Att suggested.

As the group stood together, Kyle watched from the back. "What're you waiting for?" Att looked back and said, "Get your ass over here!" Kei added. They all huddled together, and the click of the camera was louder than expected. All their faces were curled into smiles, and it turned out to be a perfect picture.

As others were busy talking about the image, Kei took his chance and said to Naveah, "Hey! I never had the chance to say. Maybe I never will if not now." He looked at Naveah to see her smile as she put her fingers in a cross near her face and said, "I'll hear it after we get out of here. So you must tell me then, and I'll be waiting."Kei blushed as his heart thundered, desiring to touch her, but it wasn't possible.

"But ca-" Just as Kei was about to say his words, the door of the rooftop slammed open as a group of people rushed inside with panic, sweat, blood, and horror in their eyes. The most vicious one among them; probably their leader, locked the door and yelled as soon as he saw them, "Who the fuck are you? Which one of you fuckers left the entrance open?"

11. Revulsion

"Who was it?!" Their leader- Ash bellowed, his voice echoing across the rooftop as he shouted.

Tensions were running high on the rooftop as the group confronted Att and her companions. The air was thick with anger and accusation, and the atmosphere was charged with a palpable sense of danger.Ash's face was contorted with rage, and his grip on his staff was so tight that his knuckles had turned white.

Saijin opened his mouth to speak as he was the last to enter, but Att held up a hand to silence him. She knew that anything they said now could make things worse. "Why does it matter?" Att asked, her voice calm and measured. "What's wrong with it?"

"What's wrong with it?" Noelle stepped forward, her hands and dress stained with blood. "Madelyn and Annie died because of your mistakes! You have no idea what you've done!"

Naveah exchanged a worried look with Att, and it finally dawned on them what had happened. The entrance they had used to enter the building had allowed the infected to infiltrate the hotel. They were here, relaxing, thinking they were finally safe while Noelle's group had been fighting for their lives below. The gravity of the situation hit them like a ton of bricks.

"I should've killed all of you when I first saw you stepping into the hotel!" Noelle snarled, advancing on them with menace in her eyes.

Noelle's group moved forward as one, their expressions twisted with hatred and rage. Att and her companions stumbled back, their hands raised in a gesture of surrender.

"Hey, wait-" Saijin began to protest, but then someone yelled out, "Ash! There are infecteds among them!!"

All eyes turned to Kei and Kyle, who had their weapons drawn and ready to fight. The situation was spiralling out of control, and Att knew that they had to do something to defuse it.

"Hey! Stop this and please listen," she said, stepping forward to cover Kei and Kyle. She tried to convince them to work together and get out of that crisis but the group's hatred was too strong to be ignored. They urged Att and her companions to leave the rooftop and face the situation below. Ash, in particular, was incensed, and he seemed to be spoiling for a fight.

"Leave or die, I'll give you 1 minute to choose," Ash growled.

With Kyle and Kei on their side, they knew that it would be easy for them to take down Ash's group, but they didn't want a fight. They had to find a way out of the hotel, and violence would only make things worse.

"Leave or die, hm? What if we don't choose?" Kyle said as he moved towards Ash, making him stumble backward from his appearance.

"Get rid of him!" Victor, the guy standing beside Noelle shouted, inciting the group into action.

But before anyone could react, Kyle swung his bat with deadly force and struck him in the head, annihilating him instantly. The sickening sound of bone-crushing bone echoed across the rooftop, and the group was left stunned by the sudden violence.

"Kyle!!!" Naveah cried out, feeling panicked."Why did you do that!!??" Att shouted, pulling him backward by the shirt."Victor....." Ash mumbled, staring at his dead body on the ground, streaming blood. "You murderer bastard!" He yelled."Murderer?" Kyle snickered, "I'm not a human to begin with."

The situation got out of hand. It was about to become a fight among humans who desired to live but Att, Naveah, Kei, Saijin-none of them wanted a fight. However, their mind changed when Noelle pointed her gun and aimed at Att, pulling the trigger. The sound of the gunshot rang out across the rooftop. The attack happened so quickly that Att barely had time to react. All she felt was a burning pain in her arm, followed by the warm trickle of blood as it dripped down her skin. She slumped to the ground, gasping for breath. The bullet would've pierced her heart if Kyle didn't pull her."Att!" Saijin grabbed her as Kei passed by and stood beside Kyle."Kyle," he called calmly."I know. Let's have a feast." Kyle and Kei charged toward the group, ready to take them down.

But before they could reach them, the rooftop door exploded inward, and a horde of infecteds poured onto the rooftop. The group was surrounded, with no escape in sight.

"Fuck!" Ash said moving backwards.Att struggled to stand up as she felt dizzy from blood loss and Naveah wrapped up her wound quickly.The number was huge and it was on the rooftop. The situation was more dangerous than expected. They strode near the edge to climb down by the AC boxes as Kei and Kyle handled the front.Ash and his group followed Saijin since they had no other options to survive. If Kyle was there, he would've killed them. Att asked them to consider for now and continue the grudge after they survive. "Let's...let's get to the 20th floor first," Att said, wincing in pain as she climbed down on the 20th floor's AC box, grabbing onto the edge of the window. Naveah was right above her, followed by Noelled and others from her group."Saijin get down!" Naveah shouted. "I need to get Kei and Kyle." He walked away from the edge saying that.Naveah Clicked her tongue and looked down at Att asking if the 20th floor was empty. Att nodded and safely made it inside the 20th floor and locked the door. As Naveah reached there, they quietly landed on the ground, helping Noelle and her other teammates- Cassy, June, and Urie."

Saijin, Kyle, Ash, and Kei were still on the rooftop. An uneasy feeling encircled them as Noelle Peeked out of the window to check the situation above."Where are they?!"

"I'm going up!" Att said."What're you talking about?" Before Naveah could stop her, she opened the door just to face a zombie groaning right outside the room and they instantly slammed it close, feeling terror and fear."Give me your dagger," Noelle asked and Att handed it to her. She slowly opened the door and attacked the three roaming infecteds outside the room, slashing their neck in silence."We'll stay here," June said and Noelle nodded, leaving them in the room.

They walked out and went near the Stairs as quietly as possible. Att was having a hard time adjusting her steps as she was sweating and her pain was increasing. "Naveah can w-" Noelle grabbed her mouth as she was about to speak,"Shh!! There's a lot ahead."Naveah got down and they peeked from the railings to see a bunch of infecteds rushing upstairs.

"What should we do now?" Naveah whispered. Upstairs and downstairs, there were infecteds everywhere. "Are there any soundboxes in this building?" Att asked Noelle and she shook her head, "I can't tell but we might find some in the party room. It's on the 10th floor." "Let's go then. I have my phon-" Att paused as she pulled out her phone and saw the battery at 9%."

It was enough to create a distraction. They took the elevator and when it reached the 10th floor, the ping sound alerted the infecteds around it as they rushed towards it with growls and hunger in their eyes. But they weren't harder to deal with compared to the ones they've fought before.

"This way!" Noelle said as she led them towards the huge party room and locked the door, seeing plenty of sound boxes there. Att strode towards them and plugged in her phone to check if they worked and they were all good. They locked all the windows and carried the sound box on the highest cabinet. They opened the main door after plugging her phone as Naveah and Noelled stood at the two sides of the door waiting for Att to tap play. She glanced at them and nodded, before tapping the play key and jumping down to dash toward Naveah.

The music started playing at a high volume, and the infecteds outside the door immediately took notice, rushing towards the sound with growls and hunger in their eyes. The group prepared themselves, waiting for the infecteds to arrive so they could lock the door.

As planned, the music created a diversion, and groups of infecteds rushed towards the party room. The floor shook as they thundered into the room, their desire for flesh overwhelming their senses.

The room was not big enough to contain all of them, but they continued to pour in. When Att, Naveah, and Noelle deemed it was enough, they pushed the door shut, leaving the infecteds trapped inside.

There were a few more approaching at Noelle's direction but they ignored her and started banging on the door. The three of them rushed towards the rooftop and reunited with Saijin, Ash, Kei, and Kyle in the middle of the 19th-floor stairs."Kei!" Naveah rushed towards Kei, feeling reassured and relieved. The four of them reached their limit, almost passing out. Saijin smirked as he struggled to catch his breath and nodded at them, "Let's get out of here," All of them agreed and were about to leave but Ash grabbed Noelle, "I-I don't feel good," he said as he retched, leaning down. "What's wrong?" Noelle grabbed him, helping him to stand.

"Hey! Step away from him-"Just when Kei yelled out, Ash threw up blood and heaved sharply. His face and eyeballs were getting covered in black fungus, and he stopped breathing in an instant. His internal organs started dribbling out of his mouth and nose as he lay on the ground motionless.

All of them froze in terror and dread, traumatised by the horrendous scene in front of their eyes- the scene of a gruesome death that was enough to haunt them forever.

12. Selfish bond

The silence was suffocating as they watched Ash's body in front of them. The smell emitting from the dead body was horrendous. Noelle could feel her legs giving up as she slumped down, trembling."Ash....w-why??...He was ....with you wasn't he?" She said, her voice shaky, "Why is he the only one dead?"She stood up and faced them. Her eyes filled with tears and the hatred was showing. "He was infected before, what do you expect us to do?" Kyle blurted out."What?" "Look, Noelle, I'm sorry we'll explain later but let's get out of here now- "Naveah tried to take her hand but she smacked it away."Explain now!" "You're wasting time," Att spoke up from behind as everyone looked at her. She glanced at them from her left arm, grabbing them to prevent the pain and bleeding."Either come with us or stay there. Your companions are also waiting on the 20th floor."

Noelle only stared at them for a moment and took a deep breath trying to swallow her emotions. It was a game of life and death, she couldn't wait for a person who was already gone. She fixed her mind and agreed to get out of that place with them.They managed to rescue June and Urie from the apartment, but on their way down to the first floor, the music abruptly stopped, and the elevator opened to reveal a horde of infected, squirming and writhing in an attempt to reach the source of the music.

"Stay behind us!" Kei yelled as he and Kyle charged forward, digging their weapons into the mass of bodies. The infected were like hungry rats, launching themselves at the group with savage ferocity. All of them put out their weapons, shooting from a distance to create a path out of that but it was hard.

The hunger inside Kei began to rise, his vision turning red. The urge to feed was consuming him from within, and he could no longer resist. He sank his teeth into an infected, ripping its neck apart like a chicken leg, and began to feast on its flesh. One by one, in a row, he tore into the infected, devouring their flesh with savage abandon.

Everyone stared in horror, unable to look away from the grisly scene unfolding before them.

"Kei!" Att called out but he didn't respond. "Crap! He's out of it." Kyle said, "Go after Kei, the line is clear but be careful." With worried expressions, the group slowly moved through the line Kei had created after devouring so many. He didn't look human anymore, rather like a demon, who might consume them as well.Naveah ignored what Kyle said and moved forward to make Kei return to his senses. She found a dirty rag on the floor and threw it at Kei from a distance to convert his attention, and it worked as Kei turned to Naveah. But his gaze wasn't the same anymore, his blurry eyes revealed his lifeless behavior as he strode towards Naveah while she froze at her place from shock. Just when he was about to bite apart Naveah's flesh, Saijin wrapped his mouth with the belt to prevent him from biting and Att blocked his hands with the baseball bat and yelled out, "Kei! Stop it. Get a hold of yourselves!"

He was strong for them to pin him down as he kept shoving both of them away. Their words weren't reaching him. Naveah was there paralyzed by the scene of Kei, she was out of thoughts, actions, and words. She knew this day would eventually come but she still couldn't accept it. None of them did. "We need to get out of this place!" Urie ran out of bullets, "There's a lot coming." "I didn't see any end to this! Just kill him and start moving." Noelle said, trying to clear the way. Att's red eyes blazed with fury as she glared at Noelle, hearing her words, "I dare you to utter another bullsit. He's my brother!" Noelle scoffed, flashing a smirk on her face, "Your brother, huh?" She laughed loudly and everyone's gaze turned towards her, "I had to leave my whole team and Ash...." She looked at Att, aiming her gun at Kei as she uttered, letting a teardrop slide by her cheeks, "Ash was my fiance!"

The moment Noelle was about to pull the trigger, Naveah moved from her spot and dashed towards her, pushing her backward as the bullet went astray, making her stumble and fall right in front of an infected, who didn't spare a second before tearing her arm off. She didn't get a chance to scream, it was one blood bath after another. "You're all murderers!" June screamed out. His hands trembling as he observed Noelle getting devoured while Urie got behind him to cover his eyes. "It's you who should've died." Urie cursed out with a grasped voice, his face wet from tears and dirt, "You'll have a worse death than us, after facing how it felt to lose your beloved people. Just die you murderers!"

Urie and June didn't put up a fight anymore. Out of bullets, hope, members, and reasons to keep on living, they hugged each other before the zombies launched at them to tear them apart for their feast.

Naveah, Att, and Saijin watched with pain and guilt in their eyes. They had nothing to do. Naveah stared at her trembling palms as she felt her eyes turning blurry from tears. She only wanted to make her lose the shot, but that had turned into a 'death'. She killed a person for her team member. Kei was still struggling to free himself from their grip.

"Tch! This is the only thing I can do!" Kyle said as he strode over and hit Kei's head with his baseball bat to make Kei fall on the ground motionless. "What the fuck did you-" Att was about to stab Kyle but he explained, "He's alive. I only knocked him out. He's still there. Let's leave first, I've found a way." Despite whatever happened at that building, they had to leave everything behind and move on to escape that hell, carrying the hatred, guilt, and regret with them. It was once again the five of them.

"Let's get to the opposite side of the city." Saijin had to break the silence, "We're in the south. Let's move to the North side of the city. I have a feeling that part might be a little safe." No one responded to his words until Att said, "Just go anywhere with medical treatment."Saijin nodded and they headed towards the North. As they drove out of that area, no one spoke a word. The horrible moments and deaths kept haunting them as they just couldn't do anything but hope for that nightmare to end but there was no end.

As they looked out the window, the sight of the drones flying overhead filled them with a sense of dread and hope-lessness. They couldn't blame the government anymore; their situation was the result of their own mistakes and choices. It felt like a test of humanity that they had failed.

After hours of driving, they finally reached the northern side of the city. It was no different from the South, but at least it was quiet. The infected hadn't noticed them yet, and they were grateful for the moment of respite.

Saijin pulled the car to a halt in front of an empty school building. As they stepped out, they couldn't help but notice the signs of fighting in the classrooms. It was a grim reminder of the reality that had happened there.

"I found the infirmary," Naveah said softly, leading Kei inside while the others searched for antibiotics.

Att slowly removed the cloth wrapped around her arm, revealing a worsening injury. She winced in pain as she examined it, her heart sinking at the sight. She knew it was a bad sign, but she tried to hide it by applying some antibacterial ointment and bandages.

"Do you need help?" Saijin asked, pulling back the white curtain to check on her.

"No, I'm good," Att replied, forcing a smile as she looked over at Kei, who was lying down in front of Naveah.

"Where's Kyle?" she asked, trying to change the subject.

"He went to check around for something useful," Saijin replied, dressing his own wounds.

As Att grew silent, Saijin spoke up without looking at her. "Don't hold onto it. Forget about what happened and keep moving forward."

Att scoffed, looking out the window. "As if it's that easy."

"Att!" Naveah called out as Att turned to see Kei waking up. She quickly made her way over to him, followed by Saijin.

"Are you feeling okay?" Att asked, concern etched on her face, as Kei tried to sit up, clutching his hand to his forehead.

"I..." Kei began, but his words were coming out jumbled and incoherent.

"Take it easy," Saijin said, trying to calm him down.

Kei closed his eyes and took a deep breath before looking at them. "Guys, I really..." He paused, squeezing his eyes shut and reopening them before taking out the gun from his waist and handing it to Att.

"What...what are you doing?" Att looked at him with a smile and a confused expression.

"I really....want you to fulfill my last wish..." Kei struggled to speak clearly as the horrible liquid spilled out from the corner of his lips.

"Lie down! Stop talking!" Naveah said with panic, moving to push him down.

"Don't...Don't touch me. Listen...Argh!" Kei coughed and clutched his head tightly, and they heard him yelping in pain.

"Get back!" Saijin said, covering Att and Naveah. He motioned for them to move away, seeing Kei turning into one of them. His groaning was unbearable to hear.

"What's wrong?" Att said, refusing to understand the situation.

"Att! Please shoot. NOW!" Kei yelled out, trying to fight himself from going berserk.

"Get a hold of yourself! You'll be fine! There's no way I'd-" Att started to protest, but Kei interrupted her.

"Sister! Please! Urgh...Kugh!!" He gasped, curling up his head as the sound of his bones twisting could be heard clearly. He cried, but the tears were blood sliding down his chin as he looked at them, forcing a smile. "Let me die while I'm still sane. I'm infected, Att. Now...Fulfill your words."

Kei wanted to be freed from his hellish existence, his expression conveying nothing but a nightmare. He had been preparing himself for this day when he was suffering every second without showing it. The way he was twisting up was too much of a cruel sight for them to behold. Being unable to bear further, Att pointed her gun with her shaky hand, feeling her body turn cold slowly. She couldn't keep her aim steady as her vision got blurry from tears, and finally, she was forced to pull the trigger. The sound of the gunshot filled the air, like the growl of hell itself, covering the sound of her quivering voice when she muttered, "We'll meet again, brother."

13. Another parting

The hole on the forehead, created by the bullet was vivid, and so was the black blood oozing out of it, just like other infecteds. Kei's body rested on the floor, cold and silent, his lips slightly apart, there was no sign of breathing. He was freed from the pain. The gun fell from Att's hand as she slumped down and touched the ground with her forehead, clenching her chest tightly. It was painful for her to scream loudly as she vibrated from anguish. She had to end her own brother's life with her own hand. Saijin stood frozen, jaw clenched, struggling to contain the overwhelming emotions that threatened to consume him. He knew what she was feeling since he also had to do something like that. Naveah's hopes and wishes all shattered into pieces right that instant. She was no longer looking forward to escaping that horrible caged city anymore. All her eyes saw was the dead body of her ambition.

Kyle was far away as he rushed over hearing the gunshot and halted after seeing Kei on the ground. He sighed, "So he really did leave before me," he said in a low voice. No one could read his expression since his face was covered in bangs as he looked down.

Time kept passing by. Every second was like the hour of the hades and every breath was as painful as being stabbed in the heart. They went silent as the sky got darker. Saijin and Kei took their time, safely burying Kei near the courtyard of the school building, which was probably a garden before but not anymore.

Att's mind was numb as she stared blankly at the ground, her eyes dry from the tears she had shed. She felt lost and alone, unsure of what to do next.Revenge? It seemed pointless now that her own brother was gone. Live? With whom? It all felt so meaningless without anyone by her side. And achieve a goal? To show whom? There was no one left to show.

Amid the deadly silence, Kyle sat beside them, his expression unreadable behind his long bangs. He pulled out two crumpled pieces of paper and spoke softly.

"Here," he said, holding out the papers. "Kei asked me to give you this the other day."

Att's heart skipped a beat as she recognized the familiar italic round alphabet on the page. It was Kei's handwriting. She took the papers from Kyle's outstretched hand and unfolded them carefully, afraid they might crumble to dust in her hands.

The pages contained his words-

If you're reading this then probably we didn't make it out-side the city as expected. This fungus isn't a joke since it had already taken over me. I wish to die before I become one of them or harm any of you. Well, I don't know if I did but anyway, Att. Don't give up. All of you. Just because a member died doesn't mean there's nothing else ahead. Keep living. According to my theories, there must be a cure. Escape and fetch it then use it on the other infecteds to bring them back. Since Kyle was the one who handed you this letter then he must be alive by now. If he makes it out with you. Help him first, he's a good person. And Saijin buddy, I know you're strong. Please take care of my sister and beat her up if needed, she's out of it sometimes. The fungus is weaker to heat and fire. If any of you have any wounds or scratches, be extra careful. The wind carries the germ, and it might get infected. And lastly Naveah,

After reading until that part, Att handed it over to Naveah and she continued reading.

Naveah, there are infinite words for me to say to you but, I guess it's too late and I don't want to hurt you. You're not alone so please keep on living for me and Att. I'm deeply sorry I can't keep my promise but If such a thing like second life exists, I'll dig you out and make things right between us. Ah! I deeply regret not caressing you when I had the chance, but I didn't want to do anything without your permission. And

Naveah I hope you'll be my eyes and see the perfect world you dreamt of. So, fighting everyone!

Naveah clutched the page against her chest and whimpered, "That idiot..." her voice barely audible, "He knew he couldn't make it."Stupid enough to care for a guy whom he just met," Kyle said as he squeezed his lips, refusing to feel pain.

Saijin was showing his back only, so no one saw his expression, he was silent, facing the corner.

Att's voice was commanding as she stood up and addressed the group, "We ran out of bullets, didn't we?" She strode purposefully towards the door of the infirmary and cast a quick glance around the hallway. The library beside the school was seen from the school window. There was a chance there might be survivors left in the library but they didn't wish to meet other survivors anymore.

"Let's get matches and whatever weapons we can find."

Without waiting for a response, Att led the way toward the sports ground, where a few infected were roaming around on the basketball court. She didn't bet an eye as she walked towards them without any sort of fear or anger. The others followed her and watched as she instantly swung her hand, smashing apart the head with the bat and it finally broke apart. Att stared at her palm which got a scratch from the broken wood."Close the gate," she said tersely, and the group hurried to the storeroom in search of weapons.

They managed to find a cache of baseball bats, but there were no matches to be found. Saijin closed the storeroom door and turned to the group. "We need to go to the cafeteria. I'll-"

"No," Att cut him off firmly. "I'll go there. You and Naveah guard this place." She pulled a mask over her face and opened the gate, looking back over her shoulder. "Kyle, come with me."

Kyle nodded. The gate closed in front of Naveah and Sajin as they watched the two of their backs while they walked away.

The cafeteria was only a short distance from the sports ground, but the journey felt like an eternity. The stench of death was overwhelming, and Att struggled to breathe even with her mask on. As they passed by the bodies of the students, they moved quietly and with small steps, trying to avoid making any noise.

Att turned to Kyle, surprised by his calm demeanor. "Does the smell not bother you?" she asked, but he only shrugged in response.

They rummaged through the kitchen, but all the food was spoiled and unsalvageable. The sight of it made Att feel sick to her stomach. However, they did manage to find a whole box of matches.

"Should we take the fire extinguisher too?" Kyle asked, and Att considered his suggestion for a moment. "Maybe we should. It might come in handy." She walked closer to take the matchbox in her hand, "you take that. I'll carry the box." She glanced around and counted, "All there left is ropes, shovel...Lucky if we find any wireless driller."Kyle paused to think for a moment and asked, "What're you planning?"

"Isn't it obvious? We're leaving towards the border right away."

With Kyle's help, they managed to find a bundle of thick ropes, strong enough to hold a person, some small knives, and fireworks.

As they made their way back to the sports ground, Att noticed that the infected were weaker than before, and the fungus on their faces was growing larger. The drones were also becoming fewer in number. Something was changing, but Att didn't care about understanding it at the moment, since her mind was tangled with vengeance and her only goal was to get out of the city as quickly as possible.

"You're planning on leaving right away, aren't you?" Saijin's question hung in the air when Att and Kyle arrived with their hands filled with boxes. "Yes,""It's almost night.""Even better," Att said, keeping the ropes and woods together. "That's why we found this," Naveah said pointing at the curtain cover made with steel and handles. It was meant for the huge hall room use. "We can keep our area fenced with it. Look, it can be folded." Saijin pushed it from the side and it shrank into a manageable size. Att felt reassured and even more confident after seeing that. That night might be their last night in that hellish caged city.

They didn't waste more time and moved everything inside the car to get near the border. If they failed to do anything, they planned on finding a place near the border for the night. Everything was as planned. However, Saijin pushed the paddle and the engine started, but the car wouldn't budge. "What's wrong? Is it out of gas?" Naveah said. "No! Everything's fine but the car won't move." He kept pushing the paddle. The engine roared to life, loud enough to alert the zombies. "Stop pushing it. You're literally inviting them." Kyle exclaimed as they heard groans around them, but because of the night, they couldn't see anything except for the inside of the car.

"I'll check the wheels, Naveah. Hold the torch." Att opened the door and looked at the wheel to see a plastic water pipe blocking their motion. As she looked ahead to see what the pipe was stuck with, she was left with horror, "Naveah...Lift up the torch." Att said slowly as Naveah moved the torch to reveal the lurking huge crowd of zombies right before them. The light only provoked them as they charged at Att with loud growls, spitting filthy liquids from their mouth.

"Fuck!" Att exclaimed as she moved backward, quickly putting on her mask. Kyle and Naveah jumped out of the car and tried to cover her as she struggled to remove the pipe from the wheel.

"Is it done yet?" Saijin asked urgently.

"I'm trying!" Att winced in pain as the wound on her arm reopened, and blood began to flow."Hurry!" Naveah yelled, trying to keep up with Kyle.

"We're surrounded!" Kyle said, his voice filled with urgency.

"Wha-what do you mean?" Naveah asked, confused."You can't leave at this rate. The car will be smashed to pieces. I can see their numbers, which you can't,"

"The pipe is off! Saijin, start-" Att began to say, but Kyle cut her off.

"Try to hold on for a bit!" he said, handing her a baseball bat and rushing away from the car.

"Where are you going? Argh!"Att cried out, trying to fend off an infected that was attacking her.

"Get inside the car, and Saijin starts right when you hear the fireworks. There's no time," Kyle yelled back, disappearing into the darkness.

Saijin nodded, understanding Kyle's plan. "What are you planning?"Att asked, her eyes fixed on Kyle's retreating figure.

Kyle didn't answer, but ran further away, taking the fireworks with him. He lit them, placing some downwards and some upwards. Within seconds, they started to explode with loud sounds and flashes of light, attracting the zombies toward Kyle's direction. They rushed towards him like a herd of wild bulls, leaving the car behind.

Saijin quickly started the engine, and the car lurched forward. "Wait! What are you-Kyle is right there!" Att said, looking behind from the back window. She could see Kyle's figure standing under the firework light, vividly illuminated.

Even though Att was far away, she could read Kyle's lips saying, "You all escape on my behalf. I'll fight until I become one of them here and.....farewell.."

14. Descent into obscurity

As the car accelerated, Kyle faded from their view, receding into the distance as they pushed forward towards their destination—the Northern barrier. Kyle knew he would inevitably undergo a transformation soon, which was why he had made the selfless decision to stay behind and clear the path for the rest of the group. The night grew darker, mirroring the heaviness in their hearts. The uncertainty of survival weighed heavily on them all, as they couldn't predict who might meet their demise next. The looming threat of the terrifying fungus overtaking their bodies was unbearable, leaving them with only two choices: to die without fighting or to die fighting.

Att's confidence decreased as she stared out the window, clutching her injured arm. Naveah's soft voice broke the silence, calling out to her, "Att... You're bleeding."

Pausing for a moment, Att replied without averting her gaze from the window, "Don't worry. It won't kill me."

Naveah wanted to say something more but decided against it, taking a deep breath instead. "How do you plan on crossing the border? The pit is deep. I don't think the rope would work."

Saijin glanced at Att and Naveah through the rearview mirror upon hearing the question. "I would have suggested taking a helicopter from the training ground, but there was none."

Att interjected, a tinge of frustration in her voice, "You think we'd be staying here if there was?"

Upon reaching the barrier, uncertainty shrouded their thoughts. They were unsure of what awaited them, but a glimmer of hope urged them to press on, even though they had already lost two members. They were merely a group of guinea pigs, chosen by those biologists. They pondered the fate of other survivors—what they were doing, how much they knew. Were they the only ones left? What was the purpose behind the experiment that risked the lives of millions? Was there truly a cure? These unanswered questions gnawed at them, tormenting their souls, with no guarantee that they would ever find the answers.

The car gradually decelerated and came to a halt, its head-lights illuminating the lifeless bodies scattered across the torn grass. Naveah broke the silence, asking, "Are we here?"

Saijin replied, his voice low, "Yes..." It was the dead of night, nearing 2 AM. The silence enveloped them, broken only by the sound of their own breathing and Att's cautious footsteps on the grass as she stepped out of the car. With a torch in hand, they directed its beam towards the towering wall before them and the deep pit that separated the two sides, mirroring the configuration of the southern barrier.

"Saijin," Naveah called out, her voice tinged with excitement, "There's a construction site."

Att and Saijin turned their attention to Naveah's left, where they saw a collection of Excavator vehicles meant for construction. Their eyes lit up with renewed hope. "God, I hope they work. Please let them work!" Att whispered repeatedly, her voice barely audible. The three of them approached the vehicles, two in total.

"Do you know how to operate these?" Naveah asked Saijin as they climbed into the driver's seat.

Saijin shook his head. "No, I've never driven one before. Are there any instruction manuals?"

Att rummaged through the seats and floor, but all she found was mud. "No."

Saijin took a deep breath, exchanging one last glance with Naveah and Att before flicking the red switch that appeared to be the power button. The vehicle vibrated and roared to life. "They work! Gosh," Att covered her mouth as relief evident in her muffled voice.

The deafening noise emitted by the vehicle would undoubtedly attract the infected, making any further progress futile. Moreover, the darkness of the night signalled the need for rest. The three of them huddled inside the car, locked the doors and settled into a tense silence.

"Tomorrow is the day. Let's do whatever we can," Naveah whispered, breaking the stillness.

Att agreed, nodding in agreement with Naveah. "The most challenging part will be crossing the pit. Once we're past that, the path should be clear, and the infected won't be able to reach us."

Saijin's gaze fixated on Att's arm, which she still held tightly. Suddenly, he spoke up. "Take it off."

Confused, Att exchanged glances with Naveah. "Hmm?"

"Your coat, take it off," Saijin reiterated.

"Why?" Att questioned.

Before she could receive an answer, Saijin moved closer, swiftly grabbing her coat and forcefully yanking it, exposing her injured arm. The bullet wound had become more than just an injury; it had become infected by the fungus. Att had managed to hold it at bay for the day since the fungus had not yet affected her brain, thanks to the wind's infection.

"Do you see what this has turned into? It's only a matter of time before it takes over your body," Saijin glared at Att, who was perspiring. She knew the severity of the situation but didn't want to confront it.

"I happen to have some Antiseptic with me. You think it would help?" Naveah suggested with uncertainty.

Saijin nodded, gesturing for her to retrieve it from the car as he pulled out a small knife, "How much pain can you endure?"Att's heart raced as she realised what he was planning. "I can't say until I experience it," she replied, her voice trembling. Naveah handed her the bottle of antiseptic, and Saijin poured some onto the knife. He glanced at Att, his gaze filled with intensity. "Feel free to bite down or do whatever you need to do, but don't make a sound."

Att nodded, gripping Naveah's hand tightly, and closed her eyes, mentally preparing herself. Saijin took hold of her hand and began cutting away the injured and infected flesh. The knife pierced through her skin, reaching the flesh beneath, causing searing pain. Att struggled to stifle her cries, biting her lips until they bled. Each cut made by Saijin felt vivid, as he continued to slice through her biceps, going deeper. It took several agonising minutes for him to completely remove the infected flesh, though, to Att, it felt like an eternity as she fought against the overwhelming urge to scream.

When Saijin finally set the knife aside, Att slowly opened her eyes and met with Naveah's worried gaze. "Are you still there?" Naveah asked anxiously.

Att nodded, her throat dry as she gulped, "Yeah..." She turned her gaze to her side, where she saw Saijin carefully wrapping her hand with a bandage. The sensation in her left arm was almost gone as if it had been severed. It made her realize the unimaginable pain that those who were devoured by the infected had experienced—the girls from before, and Noelle's group.

They needed to escape the city, but what would they do afterward? It was not like the GOV would let them in to reconcile or something. And what if... What if there was another infected city? What if there was no city left at all? The questions flooded her mind, threatening to overwhelm her.

Then, she remembered Kei and Kyle's faces. If it were Kei, he would probably say, "Let's worry about these things later. Our priority is to get out first." And if it were Kyle, he would likely declare, "Who cares? Whatever there is, I'll smash it to pieces if it gets in my way."

A smile tugged at the corners of Att's lips as an unexpected tear trickled down her cheek. She whispered to herself, "Ah! I miss you guys."

Naveah noticed her tears and asked with concern, "Does it hurt too much?"Att shook her head. "No..." She looked at her, "Just don't die on me." she requested, her voice choked with emotion.

After a moment of hesitation, Naveah opened her mouth" ....I won't."--These were the words she had spoken the night before, and Att believed in them—until that very moment in the morning, when Naveah's head was mercilessly separated from her body, but the sharp steel wire that was released by one of the infected's forceful push.

Att's eyes widened in horror as Naveah's head flew off, landing on the ground, revealing the vivid sight of her neck's cervical bones through the gaping throat. Naveah's headless body slumped to the ground, lifeless.

"Na...veah?" Att's voice trembled with disbelief as she witnessed the grotesque scene before her.

15. Out of the Hell

Everything turned dark in Att's eyes as her mind went blank and silent. She couldn't see where she was going, nor could she hear her own screams. The pain was numbed as she swung her bat relentlessly at the group of zombies before her. She had forgotten about her injured arm and continued her attack, allowing the flood of blood and tears to cloud her vision. At one point, the bat snapped into pieces under the immense force and pressure she exerted on it.Just then, one of the infected clamped its teeth onto her injured arm, immobilizing her.Att acted on instinct, determined to free herself from the creature's grasp. Ignoring the pain and fear, she made a gruesome decision. With a surge of adrenaline, she used her daggers to sever her own arm, stabbing repeatedly until the bone was completely separated. In her relentless state, she had transformed into a bloody mess, a monster fueled by overwhelming emotions. How did the situation worsen to this extent?Earlier that morning, everything had seemed fine.Att and Naveah had awoken with hope, planning to cover the pit and escape using the excavators. However, their plans were shattered when an unexpected outbreak occurred. Drones flew away, crossing the barrier, and in an instant, the area was overrun with zombies. Att and Naveah huddled inside the makeshift barrier they had brought for a shield, plotting their next move. However, the outbreak unfolded with alarming speed, catching them off guard as they desperately fought their way toward the excavator, but tragedy befell them in an instant when Naveah's life was snatched away by the unforgiving steel wire.

Now, Att resisted with a ferocity that defied her humanity, relying solely on her right hand. Her left arm continued to spurt blood, draining her strength. In the chaos, Saijin reached out and gripped her wound, shouting, "Are you trying to kill yourself too? You HAVE to leave!"

Att gradually began to regain awareness of the situation. They were given no time to grieve or mourn Naveah's loss. They had to survive. "They're plotting to explode the entire city!" Saijin exclaimed, but as he glanced at Att, he realized that trying to reason with her would be futile. She seemed lost, oblivious to her surroundings, completely unresponsive to his words. She wasn't listening to him, nor did she care, being lost in her own world of pain and anguish.

At this rate, they would both die. They needed to reach inside the excavator's chamber as quickly as possible, but the horde of infected seemed impossible to cross over. Earlier that morning, they had seen Jets flying by. There must've been an explosion in the center,r, and all the infecteds rushed near the borders to avoid the fire. There was a little time left before they blow that off too.

Without warning, Att pushed Saijin away and turned in another direction, targeting yet another infected. Saijin tried to hold onto her, but he was preoccupied with defending himself from a bite. "Att!!! Where are you-" he began to shout, but Att interrupted, her voice filled with a conclusion. "I'll handle this side. Go as fast as you can, start the excavator, and use it against them!"

Understanding her intentions, Saijin unleashed all his strength, fighting with relentless ferocity. With each shove and slice, he carved a path through the infected, inching closer to the excavator. Finally reaching it, he frantically pressed buttons until he found the one that activated the vehicle's deadly mechanism.The massive bucket of the excavator swung forward, forcefully pushing the group of zombies away from Att.

"Get on!" Saijin yelled, his voice filled with urgency, as Att swiftly leaped onto the extended stick, gripping onto its sturdy H-link. With only one hand, it was a struggle to maintain her hold. It was only then that she winced in pain and the realization hitting her that her left arm was gone.

Saijin was distracted with crushing the infected that he had failed to look ahead until Att's urgent shout broke through his focus. "Look in front!" But it was too late. The excavator had already collided with a tree, crashing down close to the pit, causing a mass of infected to tumble into its depths.

Blinking his eyes open, Saijin struggled to respond to Att's hushed voice. "Are you alright?" she asked, concern lacing her words. He could barely muster a reply, his voice barely audible, as he attempted to rise and noticed a shard of glass piercing his hand.

"I'm sorry. I don't have antiseptic," Att apologised, handing him a piece of cloth from her to stop the bleeding. Peering through the broken glass, she scanned their surroundings for any approaching infected. The overturned car provided a barrier, shielding them from the relentless zombies.

Att's body grew cold from the substantial blood loss, and she sighed as she leaned against the broken chair behind her. "We need to take the second excavator," she suggested, pointing towards the one closer to theirs. "Luckily, this crash brought us close to it."

Saijin nodded, cracking his neck and taking a deep breath. Both of them teetered on the edge of exhaustion and despair, but they clung to the sliver of hope that remained. After a few minutes passed, they mustered the strength to move forward, their progress slow but resolute to avoid attracting the infecteds. They safely made it inside the cab. "Is there no way to use it without sound? Those things will start attacking again." Att said."No, it's an engine Att," Saijin said as he turned it on and the bottom roller started moving toward the pit. Att pulled out the ropes and crowbars as they waited for the bucket to reach the wall. All of a sudden, they heard noises from outside and looked behind to see the jets flying around. Then the loud explosion sound reached their ears. They were exploding in the last area-Northern side. Att and Saijin needed to escape before everything burned down. Suddenly, they noticed a crowd rushing over, and Att cursed under her breath. "These fucking infecteds are worse than the real zombies," she muttered, scanning the area to see how close they were.

"Att, can you climb with one arm?" Saijin asked, looking concerned.

Att shook her head, glancing at her injured hand. "I'll wrap the end of the rope around my waist. That should work, right?"

"....Right! I'll climb first, then," Saijin said, taking the crowbars and opening the door. They slowly made their way across the excavator's dipper, heading towards the wall. As they approached, they realised that the pit was deep but not very wide.

With one crowbar clutched in her right hand and the rope securely tied around her waist, Att watched as Saijin prepared to climb. They exchanged a nervous glance, their hearts pounding with excitement and fear. They were finally leaving this place behind.

Saijin took a deep breath and looked up at the sky. "Come right after me," he said before jamming the crowbar into the wall. The cement was weaker than he expected, probably because it had been built in a hurry.

Att watched as Saijin began to climb, edging his way up the wall. She moved closer, preparing herself for her turn. Despite her exhaustion and injuries, she refused to give up at that point. But just as she jammed her crowbar into the wall, the cylinder beneath them started to shake, and she heard the furious growls of the zombies behind her. They had already been attracted by the noise, and some were getting dangerously close. Some even fell into the pit as they stumbled blindly after the sound.

Despite her best efforts, Att couldn't climb up in time. The shaking caused by the moving cylinder made it impossible for her to hold on, especially with her injured arm. She knew that if she had continued to climb, she would have dragged Saijin down with her. Looking at Saijin, she pulled out the crowbar from the wall. "No, what are you planning? No, no, no, don't do it! Att-" Before he could finish, Att put on a smile and cut off the rope with the crowbar.

"Go!" She cried out, "I implore you! Do anything you can to avenge us!" she yelled with all her strength as the zombie jumped on her, sinking its teeth into her shoulder. She didn't put up a fight as she lost her balance, falling down the pit while fixing her gaze on Saijin, who was yelling her name.

As she fell, she recalled Kei, Naveah, and Kyle's faces. And the memories they'd shared. She was going to join them.

Before she could realise, how far she had fallen, everything turned dark in Att's mind.

"Fuck, fuck, fuck, fuck!" Saijin was devastated, stabbing the wall with the crowbar and clenching his teeth. Tears streamed down his face as he realised that he was now the only survivor. He had known that a situation like this could happen, but he had no idea the pain and emptiness he would feel. It was the first time he had ever felt this bad after losing comrades, and his body burned with a desire for vengeance.

After taking a deep breath and clearing his vision, Saijin began to climb. Another jet flew overhead, releasing a bomb that set everything on fire. The impact shook Saijin as he kept climbing, his muscles rippling and sweat clearly visible under the orange light of the flames behind him.

He finally reached the top of the barrier, standing on his two feet as the city lights before him reflected in his eyes. In front of him was a beautiful city, and behind him was a hell burning in flames, filled with painful memories. Saijin was the only one who made it out alive from Southern Caroline, making the sacrifices of his comrades.

When he noticed a helicopter flying towards him, he switched his gaze, took a deep breath, and boxed up the emotions and memories inside his heart and mind. He knew what he had to face from then on. Dying was easy, but living was the hardest quest.

The start of the Conclusion

"**A**s expected, you were the only survivor," a man said, swiftly jumping out of the helicopter and landing beside Saijin. He handed Saijin a jacket. "Let's go back, Dr. Saijin. Sir is dying waiting for you," he said with a mischievous smile on his face.

Saijin nodded and took one last glance at the city before getting into the helicopter. "I need you to send some men to retrieve something in there," he said to the man sitting next to him.

"Sure. Anything you say, Dr. Saijin," the man replied.

As the helicopter lifted off, Saijin couldn't help but feel a sense of survivor's guilt. He had made it out alive, but at what cost? He closed his eyes and said a silent prayer for his fallen comrades, vowing to never forget their sacrifice, and whispered to himself, "I'll bring you back. The revenge play needs its audience."

www.ingramcontent.com/pod-product-compliance
Lightning Source LLC
Chambersburg PA
CBHW070448170726
48291CB00005B/1650